CW01066467

# 10
# Days of
# Freedom

Maurice Powell

The Book Guild Ltd

First published in Great Britain in 2018 by
The Book Guild Ltd
9 Priory Business Park
Wistow Road, Kibworth
Leicestershire, LE8 0RX
Freephone: 0800 999 2982
www.bookguild.co.uk
Email: info@bookguild.co.uk
Twitter: @bookguild

Typeset in Aldine401 BT

Printed and bound in Great Britain by CPI Group (UK) Ltd, Croydon, CR0 4YY

ISBN 978 1912575 251

British Library Cataloguing in Publication Data.
A catalogue record for this book is available from the British Library.

# Preface

## 2209

The world's population stands at five billion.

Eleven men escape from an area known as a Work Zone, once a prison. There are many such places, unknown to the general public, across the world, each with its own purpose.

But the imprisoned men had committed no crime.

They had been genetically engineered for one purpose only: to carry out manual work for (and on behalf of) their superiors.

Over the years, though, and through subterfuge, the eleven men had managed to collect various odd scraps of information about the outside world until, one day, they made their escape under the fences wandering through the countryside, just south of Birmingham, England, through woods, fields and along the towpaths of the canals, meeting others living out there in the open – who tell the men of the things they'd experienced. Pursuing them, and hot on their trail, was a party of Work Zone guards, high-ranking officials from Whitehall, England, and two academics from Oxford University: a husband and wife team renowned for their pioneering work in psychoanalysis.

Their remit was simple: the fugitives must be stopped at all costs (questioned, if others were involved in plotting the escape, and then killed), for the public cannot know and must never know what happens in the work zones.

Eleven had escaped but only ten were accounted for and out of that ten only seven had been shot; what had happened to the other three, and where was the missing man?

The survival of the rest of civilisation's population depended on those answers.

# 1

It was doubtful if anyone travelling along this part of the road had given the woodland that edged the road for the last kilometre or two a second thought, even less so, the equidistant rain-splattered Warning Notices fixed at intervals along a rusty old perimeter fence that encircled the entire area behind.

Was it there to keep out prying eyes or to ensure that those imprisoned within its walls remained firmly out of sight?

Beyond the woodland, overgrown with brambles and ferns, lay another fence, similar to the first, separated only by gates.

This led on to a wide open space and a two-storey building which, in turn, led on to a narrow lane alongside a canal.

Both the fences and woodland surrounded an area separated into various plots of cultivated land, like huge allotments.

Nearby stood five rectangular buildings (together, forming a large circle): each roughly two hundred and fifty metres in length; one hundred metres wide and having fourteen floors (with its own special purpose).

There were machine shops, stores, dormitories, a cafeteria, kitchens and recreational areas.

The guards' quarters were separate, located at the top of each building, where there lived one hundred men and ten armed guards.

The guards worked in shifts (and were supervised by a captain and a sergeant) with two patrolling the building, in case of trouble. Yet no-one could recall if there had ever been any.

The whole area, like many over the country, had been turned into prisons many year ago, but what it was used for now was of no concern to outsiders.

And so the story begins.

It was the end of May and just starting to warm up after a long cold winter. A small group of men were making the most of the morning sun, just talking (even though it was only 06:40, there were other groups milling about before having to start work).

Like every other man in the Work Zone, they were known by a single name. There was Jim, the electrician; there was Joe, the storeman; Mark and Phil were gardeners; Jacob, the chef; Leo tended the livestock; and Ken, Mike and Len were machinists.

Normally there were nine of them in the group. This morning, however, there were only eight. One was missing.

The eight men seemed pre-occupied: looking out aimlessly towards the ring of trees in the distance. Yet it wasn't the trees that had caught their attention, but a small gap in between a few of them that had been felled overnight by the strong gale.

One of the men seemed to be pointing to something far beyond the trees, though.

The men's interest grew stronger.

Later, two others would join the group that would make up the whole party of escapees.

In between the fallen trees, they could just make out occasional flashes of light, as if something was moving at speed and caught by the morning sun. To these men who had never saw, yet alone been beyond the ring of trees, it was fascinating.

It started them thinking, what could be out there? These men had never set foot outside the building. The only ones allowed to leave were the gardeners and the ones looking after the livestock (in their little patch of land, but only as far as the inner fence).

Everyone, including the security guards, were all prisoners. Yet they had committed no crime. Neither did they know why they were there, other than it was regarded as normal for as long as anyone could remember. It wasn't too bad. They were warm, dry and well-fed, but they were only allowed to read and watch what they'd been told to read and watch. Over the past few decades, some of the work coming in had been packed with old books, magazines, papers; anything that could be used to protect the valuable castings.

All had print on, which was a source of information to these men, and they all began to gather and hide away every little bit, as they could be exchanged between them.

They knew the risk if caught. The punishment was 'to be put *Beyond Salvage*', which meant death (but don't they say that 'Curiosity killed the cat'?). The area had been once a prison. Now it was known as a Work Zone; for this was the year 2209. The world's population had been reduced to 5.5 billion. In Britain, it was down to just 21 million.

No-one knew what had happened (it had been kept 'Top Secret' many years ago). But did anyone care or even give a second thought to those who had died? Some said it was down to war, others said disease or famine.

People took for granted what they were told and heard but sometimes the media, when using the most modern technology, could be a diabolical weapon; it could warp men's minds and control the way they thought.

No-one knew when exactly they had begun to play with people's DNA.

First they said it for medical reasons, but shortly afterwards they found it was possible to alter a man's DNA. So these men and women were required to fill the gap left by all those who had disappeared; hence, these men were just a few of many.

To the outside world, these men living and working here were criminals, and were regarded as such: just talking machines, without logic or reasoning, or feelings. They were nothing but a necessary evil, as they were needed to produce the products that were required.

Since the unavailability of the old books and papers these men had begun to use the one thing they could, and that was to collect all these scraps of paper they could get to read, and learn without the people in authority knowing. Good or bad, the rest of the people just could not be bothered so long as they received their units (units was the currency throughout the world). But someone once said 'Let me issue and control the money of a nation then I will care not for those that make the laws, for it is I that will dictate those laws'. How true those words turned out to be, money is sometimes behind the making of some laws.

They were so shallow, no thought of what had happened, they were quite happy to believe what the government and the media said, is it not the case where (History becomes legions and legions become myths).

So whatever was put before them they believed, regarding these work zones. and if they got the products they wanted, nobody cared or would admit, or say in reality these men were as good as slaves.

So over the decades things had run smoothly for the majority of the population, but greed was always there, now some wanted more.

The whole area was self-contained, the only link to the outside world was via a little miniature railway. It brought castings in and took finished work out down to a turntable, where the lines went like a spider's web to all the buildings, and to one down a small slope which led to the large iron gates hidden by tall trees, not even the guards were allowed to go near there.

These men were isolated from everyone. Even between buildings, there was no contact to be allowed. But, like all rules, after a while everyone starts to become complacent.

Then things become lax and sloppy, but as long as the work went out on time, there wasn't any trouble from outside and everything went along smoothly. Today was no exception.

The eight were too pre-occupied to be concerned about the man hidden between the huge water tanks and the large air ducts situated on the roof. Sitting on an old oil drum, away from everyone and feeling safe enough that no- one could see, Tom enjoyed reading one of the old magazines he had found. He liked it here and today was even better. He could feel the warmth of the sun even though it was just the beginning of summer. The trees were just showing their fresh leaves.

It was only when he heard the group calling out for their missing comrade did he stop reading and put the magazine away, in a hidden compartment at the bottom of his box of tools.

The box had been given to him by a man that he had worked with ever since he came here aged fourteen, who had taught him everything, especially to keep some things to yourself.

Yet, for some unknown reason, it still hurt when he thought of that day when they came to fetch him. They all knew why and that he would not be seen again.

He looked out in the direction of the small group making sure that he was still hidden from their view.

He was stocky and of average height; his face and arms tanned from sitting out in the sun every morning. Like the other inhabitants, he was known only by a single name, not a number.

Tom grew uneasy. Something was wrong. One of the men was missing.

He turned around. The missing man was there.

Tom's blood went cold. This could be the end, he thought.

But the man just stood there, smiling at him.

The man eventually spoke.

"Hello," he said. "I'm Jim."

Standing just two steps away, Tom saw that Jim was quite tall but rather pale- skinned.

He had obviously spent too much time inside.

Jim continued.

"Don't worry," he said. "We've been watching you. We know all about your books. Your secret's safe with us."

They all knew the punishment for running to the authorities.

One had and he'd been found dead the following morning, at the foot of the stairs.

Jim motioned silently to Tom to follow him.

They made their way over to the rest of the group, who were standing far too close to the edge, for Tom's liking. Though he recognised them all, he didn't know any of their names.

Tom was uneasy about being this close to the edge even if there was a guard rail.

Seeing his concern, the men moved away from the edge.

One held out a hand in friendship.

"Shall we introduce ourselves?" he asked, holding Tom's hand in a vice-like grip.

"I'm Joe."

Tom reckoned Joe was about five foot ten, slightly taller than himself.

"I work in the stores."

Tom realised that that was where some of the odd bits of information, newspaper cuttings and books had been hidden.

With that, Joe turned to the man by his side.

"And this is Mark."

Mark was stocky and his skin was a lot darker than the others. Joe continued, hardly pausing for breath.

"And this is Phil."

Phil was much shorter than the others, yet his skin was like tanned leather: the result of working in the gardens, come rain or shine, all day long.

Joe introduced the next man.

"And this is Leo," he beamed. "He looks after the animals."

Leo was tall, skinny and red-haired.

There was something cat-like about him.

"And this is Jacob. He's the chef."

Jacob was smaller than the rest of the group, well-rounded figure and even more darker-skinned than Mark; there was something Tom liked about Jacob, his smile put Tom at ease and he could remember seeing him working in the kitchens. Joe introduced the others.

Jim had still not said a word since they had joined the others; Tom had heard them calling him Sparks and realised he was one of the electricians.

He also remembered seeing him around the workshops working on machines but had never spoken to him.

Tom had worked with the other electricians while working on machines, they all had a good word for him.

They all went over to the guard rail. One section in particular had their attention.

When Mark began dismantling the top rail, and to Tom's surprise it came away quite easily in Mark's hands, he lowered the rail slightly until something slipped out of the hollow tube.

The object that had slipped out was a small cylindrical object about 100mm long, and was made of a piece of brass; Len swiftly caught it before it fell to the floor.

Then to Tom's amazement he held It up to his eye; after a while he offered it to Jim who held it up to his eye and looking in the direction of the fallen trees after a minute or two, he nodded in agreement and offered it to Tom.

Now recognising the object as part of a lens taken from one of the cameras that covered all the building, and he had a good idea which one it had come from. Bringing it up to his eye like the others had done he was amazed at how close the distant trees appeared. Not wishing to release his new-found toy he scanned around the distant trees with all their fresh leaves just breaking out, the blue of the bluebells scattering the ground, like a blue carpet under the trees. Reluctantly he passed the lens around, so they all had a turn and when they had finished it was replaced in its hiding place.

Leo spoke first, and it would be a statement that would change not only their lives but many more.

He said "I would give anything to see what it was like on the other side of the fence."

No-one said a word.

They just looked at Leo not knowing what to say. The thought had never crossed their minds.

But now just thinking about it stirred something inside; they all knew the consequences, yet no-one had objected now that the seed was sown; it would be a hard job to put it out of their minds completely, blow the consequences. Mark asked: "Would you really give anything to see what was out there? Because if what they say on the television that we watch is even half true, it's not very pleasant what with all the fighting going on."

Before Leo could answer, Jim began to introduced the others Tom had not been introduced to: there was Ken, Mike and Len; they were machinists. And it was Ken who asked:

"Does anyone really know the truth; what it's really like; what's really going on out there? If there's any way I could go, I would. It's better than just waiting to be told you are *Beyond Salvage*."

Tom could see that they were all getting used to the idea, now that the thought had been sown, even Tom could feel something inside stirring.

From the corner of his eye Tom saw a armed security officer just stepping out of the doorway of the lift. His heart missed a couple of beats, because the man was heading in their direction; he didn't know what to do or say, why he was coming over to them.

Only when he reached the group and Jim saw him and said nothing did Tom realise that he also was one of the group, so there was need for panic.

After a while it was time to get to work; they agreed to meet after work and before they departed they looked at Tom as if they were not quite sure if he could be trusted with what he had witnessed.

Would he run straight to the governor? With that they all went their separate ways still wondering if each of them would be sent for.

Sitting at his bench trying to carry on doing his job the best he could, he couldn't stop going over and over it all again; the thought of getting out of here had never crossed his mind before this morning. He'd never even considered it before and if he could he would be there later.

What would it be like beyond the fence?

None of them knew. Since he, like the others, had been brought here as a young boy, he hadn't set foot beyond the walls, let alone the perimeter fence. The only ones that were allowed out would be the two gardeners and Leo who looked after the animals, but if they were to go near the fence there would be hell to play. They were prisoners and had no rights and according to the authorities they were machines; they had no thoughts or feelings and no compassion, that was the intention of the authorities at the beginning.

But over time and with all those bits of paper, books and magazines, their minds had developed.

If the government had any idea as to the extent, they would have certainly done something about it long ago.

However, like all authorities, after a while, they had become complacent, and security began to slacken.

Things over the years had become so lax. Not all security cameras were operational.

There had been cuts in the cost of running such places nor had there been any searches of the men's personal lockers.

But something was happening. There were rumours that the entire zone was to be closed down.

Today, visitors were coming in to inspect the buildings.

So, when they met later that day, they would discuss the idea, of arranging with others from this and the other buildings if there was any way that a few of them could escape.

A problem with that was the possibility that things could become even worse for those men left behind.

Two days later, after communicating with men from the other buildings, they waited for the answer, they didn't hold out much hope.

But, when the answers did came back, it was in the affirmative and they would get all the backing and help they needed.

On the condition that, if possible, one of the men must report back and inform those remaining there, by a signal, what had been discovered.

Someone would be waiting every morning in the hope of receiving such a signal from a specified location.

So it was agreed that everything would be in place for eleven of them to escape, sometime in the next few weeks, sooner rather than later, as rumours were bound to spread and something was going to happen.

They had heard that all those of a certain age were to be put *'Beyond Salvage'* (liquidated), in order to make way for younger workers.

**2**

About thirteen miles away, in the small village of Warwick, England, Professor John Dampier sat at his computer.

The early June sun filled the room.

His attention was drawn to his wife, Yvonne, standing in the doorway of the French windows, looking out across over their garden, packed with colour, and the River Avon, and admiring the old ruins of Warwick Castle.

The ancient castle had once been a magnificent building but now, over time, it had been stripped of everything worth taking.

Yvonne knew he was admiring her, standing there in her thin cotton night-dress. She also knew that, with the early morning sun shining upon her, John could see every line of her slim figure through the material, hoping it was having the desired effect.

Smiling to herself, she parted her legs just slightly enough to tease him a little. With her natural tan and dark tight curly hair, she was a natural beauty.

They had met when they were in their twenties, while at university as psychology students at Bristol University.

As doctors both lectured in psychoanalysis at the local university and sometimes working very closely with the police, helping in cases where people had mental problems and also when there were anxious parents worried about their child's behaviour.

They had worked together many times, John's ability to be able remember and store in his memory page after page of literature.

But despite being married for fifteen years, they had no children, having no wish or desire to go through the procedure of choosing a child in the manner that one might choose a pet.

In 2209 many children were born by surrogacy.

John and Yvonne had decided against it, but right now, John's mind was elsewhere.

Transfixed, he could make out every curve.

He knew she was teasing him, but didn't mind one bit.

It was having the intended effect; even more so when Yvonne turned around and began to walk towards him, slowly undoing the two little bows that held the night-dress in place, allowing the nightdress to fall to the ground.

He waited as she walked towards him, as naked as the day she was born.

Leaning backwards against the large old desk his pulse racing, he waited until her body was pressing against his, then letting his light cotton dressing gown fall to the floor their bodies were as one moving together in rhythm, losing control they slipped slowly to the floor.

Both lay on the floor exhausted, their bodies drained of any strength.

It had been so passionate that their bodies gleamed with perspiration.

After a while, Yvonne turned, then realising that John had fallen asleep, she let her eyes travel down his body and smiled; how quickly the mighty are fallen she thought.

Slowly she got to her feet and made her way towards the kitchen.

*Sex was thirsty work*, she thought.

While waiting for the coffee percolator to boil, her fingers began to wander over her body, down between her thighs, she felt the moistness inside, and the strong desire for more began to flow through her whole body.

Slowly she made her way back with the mugs of strong hot coffee, doing her best not to spill any, over John's naked body, she could see that he was still fast asleep.

Placing the mugs on a small table that stood nearby, she knelt down alongside the sleeping figure, filling her mouth with the warm liquid, then slowly she bent over the now limp manhood, gently washing the whole length with the warm liquid in her mouth.

It wasn't long before she felt the reaction she wanted.

Gently moving on top straddling John's naked body, she began to lower herself gently, feeling the sexual excitement making her whole body quiver, as she felt John's erection slowly filling her body.

By now John was fully awake and began to caress her breasts and nipples with the palms of his hands bringing them both even more quickly into a state of a frazzling climax.

It was just at this point in time when the room was filled with a loud buzzing.

They both realised what it was.

The communications screen on the wall began to come to life; they knew that whoever it was trying to call them this early in the morning that it must be very urgent.

Cursing, John lay on his back for a few seconds threatening to have the whole system ripped out.

"Who the fuck is that calling at this time of day?" he shouted.

Yvonne didn't say anything, just smiled to herself, leaving it to him to see who was calling.

Reaching over for the keypad, John hit one of the keys, and watched the huge screen to see who it was that would be calling at this time. It had only just gone 06:45.

After a while when the face did appear on the screen, it was a face which at first he did not recognise.

Then he realised he had seen the woman before.

It had been when he was called to the council offices in Birmingham.

What puzzled him was why she should be calling them. He had no idea why she, of all people, would be calling them at this time of day.

He also had a recollection that she held a very important and powerful job and, if he remembered rightly, she answered to Brussels alone, and was a very dangerous person to cross.

So what on earth did she want with him or Yvonne, or both?

He didn't have to wait long to find out.

Wasting no time at all she instructed them both to be in Birmingham at the council offices by 09:00 and not to be late, it will all be explained when you are here, transport will pick you both up at the station.

With that, the screen went dead.

Yvonne entered the room asking who it was that was calling this early. John said that he still could not remember her name, and he didn't know why they had been ordered to report at the council offices, just that they must be there.

After a shower, they got dressed and had something to eat, they were ready to make their way to the station, which was about a twenty minute brisk walk from their home.

Both wondered as to why they had been called so early in the morning.

As far as they knew, they hadn't done anything wrong.

On the way they stopped for a moment to think on a old stone bridge that crossed over the River Avon, as it travelled through the village of Warwick heading south.

Looking down at the fast-moving river, they could see that one of the trees, in the distance, had been felled by the heavy storms the night before, lying across the river blocking the path of anything travelling downstream.

Yvonne remembered some of the stories that she'd been told in her childhood, about this area and that it was believed that for many years, before their parents time it was a children's play area, and now it was just an overgrown piece of land with a small copse running along the river bank.

She remembered stories about the small boats that once went up and down the river for fun; now the rivers were used like the canals for the transportation of goods.

But they were kept clear and well maintained.

They continued their journey, passing the old St Nicholas Church, to the station.

The steeple still stood defiant against the elements and man. Not many people attend church these days.

At least they had the promise of a fine day.

The walk to the railway station had taken them longer than usual, because of their stop.

They didn't rush, they knew that there was still plenty of time till the train was due.

There was a hint of fine rain and a fresh breeze whistling through the station when they arrived, luckily for them the train arrived as soon they had stepped onto the platform so they didn't have to wait.

As the train sped towards their destination it was John that broke the silence first, explaining that he thought it would be nice to wander around the centre again; it had been quite a while since they had been to Birmingham.

Yvonne didn't answer.

She gazed out of the window at the forest which covered most of the land between the towns, yet every now and again, there were open fields where the crops, in a couple of months' time, would be ready for harvesting; nature in other places had once again taken over.

Occasionally the forest would be broken with ruins of buildings that had not been used for decades, then there would be a road covered and broken by young saplings or vines, or both.

She sat wondering what had happened to the buildings and all those people, that had built and lived in them all those years ago.

It was the same questions she would often ask herself whilst she was in the garden, overlooking the river at the ruins, which everyone said had been a magnificent castle in the past, but that was long ago in history and no-one was allowed to ask too many questions.

Nearing the city centre, she noticed that the ruins were becoming more scarce. Every so often she could make out people climbing over the skeleton of the buildings and running amok through the rubble.

The rain eased, she noticed men demolishing a building and carefully putting the materials aside.

When the train pulled into the station, they were met by a young man, who explained that he was there to ensure that they made their way straight to the council offices, as everyone was there waiting for them.

At the council offices they were escorted into a private room, whose walls were panelled from floor to ceiling and covered with large oil paintings, all by various artists. There was one that took John's fancy: it was a huge painting of a square full of people dressed in all types of clothing, everyone going about their business, it reminded him of Venice.

Both John and Yvonne were impressed. Yvonne shook her head, as if to say that she didn't understand what this was all about either. In the middle of the room stood a huge table.

Placed around it were about thirty upholstered chairs.

They hadn't the time to count.

The doors opened and five smartly dressed men and two women entered. John recognised one as being the woman that he'd seen on the screen. She appeared to be in charge, yet it was the other woman that was getting all the attention.

Her eyes, like a cat's, were green; her hair red, and her two-piece suit was tailor- made to fit her figure perfectly. She was clearly aware of the attention she was getting.

The five men were like bees around a honey pot. A map hanging on the wall, just behind the door that they had entered, caught John's eye, it was a map of Britain, Europe.

It was covered with numerous different coloured

markers; curious he made a move to go and inspect it more closely.

One of the five men noticed John's interest and approached him.

He was a short stocky man and, by the way he dressed, had an air of authority about him.

The man's eyes and hair were charcoal-black; his beard well trimmed; his accent, a mixture of Asian and English.

He was obviously well-educated, sent to one of the best schools no doubt: Eton, maybe.

He turned to John:

"What do you think of the map?" he asked.

"I've no idea," replied John.

The stranger was about to explain what all the different colours meant when they were summoned to join the others and were told they were all about to leave. John looked at Yvonne, to see if she had any inkling as to where they might be going.

She shrugged her shoulders. She didn't know.

The woman in charge introduced herself as Margaret Storrs.

Before she introduced the others, she said that she had been instructed by headquarters, in Brussels, to reorganise this area, and that is why you are all here to help, with your expertise.

It hadn't escaped Yvonne's notice that all the time Margaret had been talking, she hadn't stopped looking at the other woman, who she now introduced as Dr Pearson.

Both were very attractive women. Turning to the

gentleman that had spoken to John, she introduced him as Mark Sykes and that he was the Director of Production covering the whole of Britain.

Britain was part of the European state; the other states were the American, African, Asian and Russian. Every state had its own government that met together, twice a year.

The man smiled at this and gave them a little bow before she quickly carried on not wanting to waste any more time than was necessary, introducing the other two, she made no attempt to introduce a man that stood alone at the far end of the room.

But the stranger, who had made no attempt to mix, didn't bother. He stood well away, by himself. He wore the uniform of a captain of the security forces, they were informed later.

With all the introductions over, she started to explain why they were there.

"Where we will be going today," she kept looking at John and Yvonne while she was speaking, "must be kept to yourself. No-one, not even your closest friends, must ever know these places ever existed or the men that live there, or what we do there is that clear to all of you?"

"Are you telling us, that there are places where people are locked away for no apparent reason and will spend most or all of their lives there no one and no knows that they exist?"

"Do I understand these instructions correctly, and you want us to help you pick which ones we think are no longer of any use to you?" John couldn't hide the anger in his voice.

She carried on as if he hadn't said a word, but the look and her next words told both of them that they must be careful.

"Yes," she replied. "There will be some unpleasant work ahead and there will be some of the men that will be *Beyond Salvage*."

Yvonne looked puzzled.

She asked: "What do you mean: *Beyond Salvage*?"

John could no longer hold back his anger. He was about to say something, when the man who had spoken to him came over.

"Those that Margaret is talking about," he explained, "They are just talking machines."

It was at this point Yvonne could see the anger in John's eyes so she quietly placed a hand on his arm before he said something that they would both regret. It was at this point that a young girl dressed in a maid's uniform came in through the huge doors and without saying a word handed a note to Margaret Storrs, who informed them that their transport had arrived.

Leaning over, Yvonne whispered into John's ear:

"We've been saved by the bell."

They still did not understand what they were supposed to do. John had began to feel a little uneasy about the whole thing, specially the remarks about the machines that talked, then there was the one about putting them *Beyond Salvage*. What on earth was that all about, he dreaded to think.

Neither he nor Yvonne relished the idea of what lay ahead; nor did they have any idea what Margaret Storrs had been talking about. They didn't want to know either. They'd sooner be back in Warwick.

Outside of the building just by the main doors the group stood enjoying the warm sun, watching the people sitting at the table outside a restaurant opposite while they waited.

They were not kept waiting long before they were all packed into a small people carrier and were soon on their way, moving slowly along the pedestrianised area , then moving faster as they joined narrow half empty roads, but soon the smooth roads turned into narrow lanes.

Margaret began to explain where they were heading and for what reason John's and Yvonne's presence was required, at all times, as they were both specialist in human behaviour and their expertise would be most useful.

Along with the expertise of the other members of the group, of which only Sykes had said a single word.

Nor had they yet been properly introduced, it would be interesting to know where their line of expertise lay.

As the people carrier rocked along what now had turned into a very muddy track, it turned off one of the main routes into and out of the city, and by now everyone was feeling a little concerned where they were being taken.

Like all others, Birmingham was no longer regarded as a city; only London was known as a city because cathedrals were things of the past, one's religion depended on one's conscience.

Along the sides of the track Yvonne could make out more of the ruins amongst the trees; in some places they had to slow right down to push through where the trees had overgrown the muddy lane.

At one point, one of the group asked why had they come by this 'bus' rather than by train.

There was no answer for that.

It was obvious there would be no stations around for miles; whoever it had been that had made the comment decided that it would be safer not to press the point. John was now looking more at the second of the two women. He had seen her before on two previous occasions but had thought nothing of it, and even though she hadn't said much until now, he guessed that she would have a large say on what happened today.

She was very attractive with her long red hair and those brilliant green eyes that seemed to be able to go right into one's mind, he imagined that she was about 190cm tall, but when she had looked in their direction he felt uneasy having the feeling that you had to be always on your guard when you were in her company.

Yet she and Margaret Storrs seemed to get on well together so all they had to do was to stay clear of both of them.

Soon even the lane they were travelling on became overgrown and the 'bus' had to slow down even further.

After a sharp turn, it came to a stop in front of two

large metal gates. Sitting there taking it all in: the huge gates, the canal that was less than a metre away, the bank opposite looked so overgrown it would be impossible to get through.

Either side of the gates stood a row of two-storey buildings. Between the buildings and the path that ran along the canal was a garden full of brightly laid flowers that brightened the whole area up.

They could see that the canal had been opened out wide enough to allow narrow boats to be able to turn around then continue in either direction, along the side of the lane facing outwards a sign signifying that these buildings were detention quarters.

They sat there for what seemed like an eternity, before there was any sign of movement, then the gates slowly began to open.

What lay before them even Margaret seemed to be taken by surprise at the site: an open space surrounded by several buildings laid out in a group of multi-story buildings, the likes John had never seen neither had Yvonne by the way she let out a little gasp.

"What is this place," he asked the man who had been introduced as Mark Sykes, the Director of Production, who had been on the point of explaining the significance of the map with all the different coloured markers.

"Do you remember that map you were interested in, back there?" he asked. John nodded.

Satisfied that everyone was listening, the man continued: "Did you notice all the different coloured markers? Well, the colours represent what the different zones produce. This one has a blue marker, meaning it's a machining zone."

"What are the pink markers for?" John asked, wishing he hadn't before the question was out.

The man smiled benignly.

"Not all the zones are for machining; for instance, the pink indicator shows a Maternity Zone."

It took John a while before he realised the significance of what the man had just said.

"Are you telling me that the people in these zones have been especially bred to work here?"

The man's expression hardened. He looked at John as if he was an idiot.

"Let me explain something that seems to be bothering you, John," he said. "After the loss of so much of the population, there wasn't enough people left to do the work required for civilisation to survive. There were enough sperm and eggs frozen to give us a fighting chance. Whatever happened all that time ago caused chaos and put civilisation back centuries. So what would you have done?"

"This is not the only production zone."

"There are many more all over the world, producing anything from soap to automobiles, anything that is required by the likes of you and I, all sorts of things."

It was then both he and John saw the looks they were getting from the two women and they knew that enough had been said.

John understood how bigger the problem it must have been. (But what had happened?)

As a second pair of gates were opened, they were met by a small man wearing a smart grey suit who introduced himself as the governor, he led them up a narrow path following a small gauge railway line, that led up to some kind of turntable system and from there the lines went off to terminate at each building.

One of the men of their group began to study a folder which he had been carrying.

A second or two later, he pointed in the direction of one of the buildings. Now it was Mark Sykes' turn to ask a question: "Was there any reason why they were going to this particular one?"

Margaret Storrs explained that there was no reason other than they were told to check just one, and the others would be treated equally. John asked: "What are we supposed to be looking for anyway?"

Again it was Margaret who answered wishing to see what their reaction would be, explaining that "their work here was to see if this zone could be closed or the workforce could be reduced without it in any way affecting production here or anywhere else, which of these men would be suitable to be trained in other things?"

With that she headed towards a small door guarded by a single armed guard. Seeing the little group heading his way the guard promptly opened a small door to let them through.

The door was by the side a much larger roller door where the narrow track entered; the guard ushered them through. When they all were in, he followed till they came to another door, where he stopped and locked the door behind them and stayed by the door, making sure that no-one left or entered, while they continued their guided tour around this strange building.

Now it was the turn of another man, who had been waiting for them just inside the last door, who told them that he was the general manager of this one building, he asked for some identification before they would be permitted to go any further; they each showed the passes that they had been given when they had first arrived at the gate.

Once he was satisfied that everything was correct, he began to guide them through the maze of passages.

As they walked on through the buildings he explained what kind work was carried out on each of floors, but as they passed through each floor the men they encountered didn't seem to be too concerned with their arrival.

Yet when they reached the machine shop the men stopped what they were doing and watched as the party was taken to each machine in turn, whereupon the attending operator explained what the machines were doing.

Not having the slightest interest what the men were doing, John stood back, more interested in the men and the interest being paid to the three women. The looks were more than just curiosity.

They seemed to understand the differences between the group especially Dr Pearson.

Next stop was the toilets and bathroom area, then

someone asked where do these men sleep, but their guide just carried on as if he had not heard just said the next stop was the roof.

Here they were told was the men's recreation space, it was here that they could do whatever they wanted within reason, and in their own time.

Walking right up to the edge, John looked down at the area below between the buildings and the first thing he noticed was that the whole area had been sectioned off into segments and had been cultivated.

When he asked about it he was told that certain men were gardeners, and a man looked after some small livestock, they produced most of their own food. It was then that someone asked the cost for each man's keep.

Margaret said: "It's more than their keep that was important here," and without another word she stormed off in the direction of the lifts.

Yvonne had noticed one of the men standing hidden away behind the huge water tanks, making it look like he was busy, but it was the way he had been watching them, that concerned her, and she could have sworn that she had seen him before down in the machine shop, just a few minutes ago.

There was something that else puzzling her. She then realised that the man seemed mainly interested in the women, not the men, yet if none of these men had ever been out of this zone let alone this building, and had no knowledge of females, or did they, why wasn't he bothered about the others of the group? As they made their way to the lift she gave this man a closer look. It didn't seem to bother him in the slightest.

He just gave a slight smile and carried on watching the small group make their way towards the lift, as if it was an everyday thing for a group of people that included women to come and wander around.

Yvonne could not tell if Margaret or Dr Pearson had noticed the man's curiosity; neither had said anything so she decided to wait till they got home then she would mention it to John what she had observed. Especially after they were told that these men had been incarcerated in here since they were just fourteen years old, and the average now was around thirty years.

As they were about to enter the lift, their guide whispered something in Margaret's ear.

John, being the closest, could only make out that something was wrong on one of the machine floors.

She quickly gave the order that they were to stop and see what the fuss was about.

Arriving at the floor, where the trouble was supposed to be, the doors opened and the sight even surprised Margaret. The floor was packed with guards and men all grouped around a man lying on the floor.

Asking what was the trouble with him, she was told by one of the guards that there had been an accident, a casting had come out of the machine and hit him in the chest.

Having pushed her way through the crowd Dr Pearson bent down to inspect what damage had been done to the poor man's chest. He was dying in agony in front of them. With the shake of her head, everyone knew that there was little that could be done.

Reaching for her bag that Yvonne had noticed had never left her side since they had met, she retrieved a little silver box that contained a small glass syringe, which she filled with a colourless fluid.

As she began to administer the fatal dose of liquid, Yvonne saw the terror in the man's eyes.

"What happen to the man's body now?" asked someone out of their group.

"Before I answer that", said the governor of the Zone, "may I explain how this place functions? First, we produce all our own energy from that smaller building with the chimney stacks, you may have seen it as you came in, right at the far end, that is our foundry where we melt down any damaged castings and scrape into ingots. Also we burn all our waste paper, scrape food etc which produces all our hot water, electricity and heating so anything that burns is feed into the furnace's."

There was not another word spoken from the little group of visitors, he had made his point and answered the question.

By the time they arrived back at the town centre it was getting late. Neither John nor Yvonne felt like talking, they had too much on their minds; as the trees and wild flowers passed them by Yvonne kept thinking of the look on the man's face as he took his last breath.

Under her breath Yvonne said, "They were just children. What have we done?" but it was loud enough for John and some of the passengers of the train to hear.

After the visitors had gone, time was getting on and as there was a shortage of castings, the men were allowed to have an early night, which they were told would have to be made up for later.

So most of the men headed for the roof to discuss the visitors, no-one had seen or witnessed anything like it before. Jim was concerned.

"If we didn't go now," he said, "it would probably be our last chance. We would never see the likes again."

# 3

The group gathered by the handrail to discuss what their next line of action should be. Tom, however, had been distracted by a series of flashes coming from the building opposite.

Most of the others didn't seem that bothered.

Only Joe reacted.

Taking a scrap bit of paper from his trouser pocket, he began jotting down a series of dots and dashes.

After a while, the flashing stopped.

The group gathered around Joe, waiting anxiously to hear what the message had said.

Then, from the old tattered book that he always seemed have in his overall pocket, Joe cross-referenced the messages that he'd received. On another piece of paper, he began to translate the message into English.

After he'd finished, he read aloud what it said.

"The message was asking us if we knew the reason(s) for the visit."

"You'd best tell 'em we don't know," said Jim.

Joe delved into his other trouser pocket and pulled

out a broken piece of mirror wrapped up in an old rag.

The sunlight was fading quickly. Joe replied to the message with a series of dots and dashes.

There was just a single flash from the other building informing them that they understood.

Jim turned to Tom:

"That's one of the ways they could correspond with the other buildings without anyone knowing what they were doing," he said. "None of us has any idea what it is either. Joe's the only one that can read and write it. They used to call it Morse code."

He continued:

"There's another way we can pass messages around, but I'll explain that some other time, OK?"

Tom looked puzzled.

"You aren't the only one that had books and papers hidden away somewhere," added Jim, making a gesture that he meant all the other groups that were scattered all over the whole roof top. Some playing games, others were just standing around talking or just getting a little fresh air before going down to their places of work.

"Every one of us here has our secrets. I'm sure you were told to never reveal your deepest thoughts to anyone, even the ones you trust most, because you never know."

A couple of days later, nothing more had been said about the visitors, nor about the closure of the site.

Everything seemed to have gone back to normal.

Not to this group though. They knew that something was going to happen.

One suggestion had began to crop up in all their conversations and in their thoughts. What had once started off as just a simple remark, made in the spur of the moment, had now become their aim: to be free, even it if was just for the one day.

It might be their last chance.

A further two weeks passed. It was coming to the end of June and still no-one had heard anything.

Tom started to think that it had all been idle talk or just wishful thinking.

Then one morning Steve, the security guard, mentioned he had heard that there had been more discussions on what the effect would be on the production of goods if this site or others around the area were to be closed down.

That would mean one thing and one thing only.

"Where would that leave us?" asked Mike. "Are they are intending to get rid of us?"

After a pause, he continued:

"What are we going to do about the idea we've been discussing over the last few weeks? I wonder if those in the other building have heard anything yet?"

Making sure no-one was watching, Joe took out his piece of broken mirror, then waited, for one of the others to retrieve their adapted telescope from its hiding place. Then with a pencil and paper he was ready to send and to receive their answer.

He positioned himself and waited for the sun to appear from behind a cloud. Tom looked on in amazement as Joe sent a string of flashes across the open space between the two buildings. A message had been sent, asking if anyone in the other buildings had heard anything.

It took a few minutes for an answer to come back.

They had also heard that something was going to happen.

They weren't sure what.

Replacing the glass back into its hiding place it was time to make their minds up once and for all. How many of them would still want to go, knowing that it would be impossible for any of them to return?

"If they were able to get out," Jim said. "I would take the risk, no matter what happens now."

Then, after talking for a while, they all decided that they had nothing to lose: either way the future did not look too promising.

"The next thing we'll have to do," said Tom, "is we'll have to inform everyone here and in the other buildings, of our intentions. This isn't going to affect just us or the ones that end up going. There'll be repercussions, once they realise that we've gone."

"I agree," said Len, "but that also means risking letting the security know what we plan to do."

"Maybe," replied Jacob thoughtfully, "but we still have to tell the people in the other buildings as well."

Two days after everyone had been informed who needed to know in this building and the other four buildings, there had still been no sign of the management having any idea what was going on.

Everyone in this building and the other four had

pledged all the help they would require, on that one promise.

So a little group got together and began to make some arrangements and plans for the escape: when, how or if it would possible to get out.

At least just getting a chance of seeing what was out there, hopefully without being captured as soon as they were out.

After a couple of weeks, everything was going fine. The weather for mid-July was unpredictable. They had found a way out through one of the ventilation ducts. Entry could be gained through one of the inspection hatches which Tom and Jim used for the maintenance and inspection of the extractor fans which would have to be isolated beforehand.

Another snag was that they had no idea how they could be sure that no-one could hear them descending down the metal duct. It would sound like a kettle drum with so many of them descending at the same time.

It was Tom who came up with the answer.

"Even though there's a ladder," he said, "it's a long way down from the point of entry. So what I do is lower myself down by a pulley system. It's quite straightforward. No-one will hear us. You'll be able to take all you need."

After a short pause, giving the others time to take in all that he had said, Tom continued.

"Then we can cross over to the other side where I would have removed a panel earlier giving us access to get to the point where we exit. I've covered the floor of the duct with old carpet and rags, but you must be very careful. There are some very sharp edges."

Another short pause.

"I've got all the stuff that we will need to get down."

But they still had no idea where they would exit the shaft.

It was Mark and Phil who came up with the answer. "We think we know where the ventilation shafts come out".

Mark started to explain that if they were right: "There would be a small drop of about three or four metres, we would drop opposite the pig sties."

He had their full concentration, as he began to describe the route they would take.

"Then we would follow the wall of the sties until we reach the chicken run, there inside we would find hidden at the back of the hen house a loose panel which backs on to the inner premature fence."

An amazed Jacob turned to Mark and asked:

"Am I right in thinking that you're telling us you've been through a hole in the fence already?"

Mark just laughed.

"How do you think we've been able to get messages and whatever is required to the other buildings? We meet those from the next building, where the fences meet and then they pass the message, or whatever is wanted, on till it gets to where it's needed."

"Another thing," added Phil. "We've been out as far as the outer fence; the area has been left for so long that the undergrowth is like a jungle, thick with young saplings and brambles, so we'll all need to wear some good thick clothes and gloves, and if we crawl along no-one will be able to see us, and in the meantime me and Mark will cut through the outer fence."

The others looked on impressed.

Tom still could not make out what it was that was bothering him about Phil and Mark; there was something about them that he could not fathom.

He noticed the machinist they called Mike looking at him. He came over and in a whisper, asked Tom 'if he had worked it out yet?' as he turned away to join the rest of the group he told Tom 'not to worry about it'.

Jim who had been listening from a little way off came over and said:

"I think we've got more serious things to think about. The number one question if we do get out is: how long do any of us think we're going to last?"

Taking Tom aside Jim explained.

"Phil and Mark not only work together, out there in all kinds of weather, left alone for hours on end, sometimes trapped in that little shack of theirs for hours. They'd be drawn together more than any of us, but don't let it bother you, you will never understand because it's the one thing we are not supposed to experience, feeling or attraction to someone else, in these places. There is no place for feelings or sentiment here.

"But don't you feel anything when one us, who you have worked with for such a long time, is taken away? And how about those females? What did you make of them? Didn't they smell nice?" asked Tom, wanting to find out if the women affected anyone else other than himself.

But the problem now was to get out, they had just heard from the other buildings that the whole zone was to be closed down very shortly so making the escape planning more important than ever.

Only two weeks after they had heard, everything was in place for the escape. Even though it was the end of July and the date for the breakout had been arranged with the other buildings to be on the 8th of August, everyone was getting nervous.

The thought of the prospect of seeing for the first time what really was out there, since being brought here all those years ago, not even stepping outside. This building had been their home since being brought here at the age of fourteen years.

But once they had stepped outside, none of them would ever be allowed back, and they all knew that each one would be *Beyond Salvage*.

But now there was nothing to lose. There was one condition that the little committees from this and from the other buildings had demanded for their help, it was the promise to all those remaining here, that they would do all that they could to let them know what it was really like beyond those fences, that's if it was at all possible.

# 4

## 8th August 2209

The time had come. Everyone knew what to do.

The plan was for Tom to go down into the ventilation duct first and ensure that the others following him knew exactly what to do once they were all at the bottom. Jim was to be next.

Being a dab hand with all things electrical, working his way through the maze of ducts would be child's play; a piece of cake.

He was to lead the men to the exit and, as Mark and Phil had said, it was just opposite the pig sties.

Their intention then was to make a break around 01:30.

That way they'd have a head start and, hopefully, time to get away.

All those that had been on the roster to do a morning shift were to be covered.

And alternative arrangements had been made.

One snag was that Steve was on security for that night, so he was the only one that could be missed; there was nobody that could be asked to cover for him. It was the chance they had been waiting for and with a little bit of luck, they may have a few hours before someone would notice that they were missing. Everyone that was to be left behind had been told to hide or get rid of any papers and books that they may have. Some of the older men had been around and collected everything, placed the items in small boxes then marking the boxes to indicate who the box belong to without giving the name away.

When all the boxes had been collected, they were taken to a place where they were to be hidden. Only a couple of older men would know where the boxes were hidden and they were hoping that those doing the search would not find anything that would implicate those that were left.

Now the time had arrived, everything was in darkness, but in the shadows the men moved silently along the passageways to a point where they had arranged to meet. Jim stood silent and Tom had removed one of the panels from the ventilation duct making it accessible, and he made his way down to the bottom to wait for the others; one by one each of the group climbed into the hole and fitted into a harness of the pulley which helped as they slowly made their descent down the ladder fitted to the inside of the ducting; they made not a sound.

Making sure the others were happy with it, when

they were at the bottom, their bags were then lowered down by the same pulley. When everyone and their gear was at the bottom of the duct, the pulley was removed and the panel replaced. It was a slow process. By the time they were all at the outside grill, it had taken forty minutes.

But there were no sound of alarms, no guards running around.

The extraction fan had been switched off and isolated, they had climbed through into a large duct that taken them straight down to the first level. Now all they had to do was to remove the outside grill, and they were all safe.

From where they were, they could see the pig sties below them, and through the blue hazy light of the moon, they could make out the hen house and the gardens giving it a look of the unreal. It would be the very first time that any of them, other than Mark, Phil and Leo, had ever been down to ground level since they had arrived.

As each man dropped to the ground they knew they had passed the point of no return, and they knew there were those watching their progress from this roof and the other buildings, wishing them luck, because they would be needing every bit of it.

The time now was only 01:45 as they had made a earlier start and the little group made their way along a narrow path, huddled together against the walls of the sties.

Now it would be up to Mark and Phil to lead them

safely through the hen house, out into the maze of young saplings and bushes, pushing their bags and equipment in front of them, they made good time. Both men had done an excellent job over the last few weeks. They had taken it in turns to crawl through brambles, nettles and young saplings, cutting a path right up to the outer fence. There they had found it to be made of angled metal bars sharpened at the tip.

Jim and Tom looked at one another, both thinking that this was going to take some time even if they chose to climb over, but they soon realised that Mark and Phil had previously loosened some of the bolts at the bottom, so the bars could be spread apart allowing the men and their bags through easily. Tom now knew why they wanted to borrow some of his tools.

By the time they had reached the outer fence it had only taken just over an hour, and just In front of them was an area of long grass, weeds and an occasional wild flowers filling the early morning air with a beautiful perfume.

Making their way through the long grass they came across something they would, or could, never of imagined. It was a long stretch of flat surface going way off into the distance in either direction.

It was Len who explained.

"This is what they use to call a road. It's how they transported goods and moved around the country. But, at this time of night, there should be nothing moving at all."

Watches were one of the things that had been allowed, so they all knew what the time was. But now they had to decide in which direction they should go. Len produced an old torn and tattered survey map. The date on the front cover was 2025. Strangely enough, he seemed to know exactly where to look on the map.

Then laying it down on the ground so they all could see, he began to explain where on the page they where, saying: "I think the different lines represent things like roads, rivers and canals; have you noticed that these have numbers?

"The one where I think we are is a number A345. It's a map of the whole area but It looks like there maybe a few changes since then," he said with a smile. Walking a little distance along the road, looking across into the dense forest that seemed to cover the opposite side of the road well into the distance, they saw what they had been looking for: a small gap in the bushes and brambles, exposing a narrow track made by a fox or a wild dog.

Making a quick dash across the open road, the only sound was their shoes on the wet surface.

Once they were safely across, Jim who had been accepted as leader, volunteered to take the lead into the darkness of the forest.

Now they had started to feel the cold chill of the night air, it would be the first time any of them would have been out of their beds at this time of night, only Mark and Phil and Leo had experienced how the temperature could drop, they knew what it could be like.

Now as they went deeper into the forest the air seemed much thicker.

The strong aroma of the unseen flora filled the dense woodland, making it difficult to breathe.

Turning this way then that, they followed the narrow track. It was hard going.

The moonlight was hidden by the overhanging branches of the trees.

Their only source of light was from Steve's torch which he had handed over to Jim, who was leading the way, guiding them over any obstacles that crossed their path.

After a while the going got easier, as they made their way through the thick undergrowth.

The narrow track suddenly opened out, into an area where several roads met.

One of the roads had a sign saying it was the A345, one which they had crossed earlier, the others only had names.

In the middle where the roads met there was an island, but here the weeds and the grass had been cut and well maintained, so they had a clear view of all the approaching roads.

Checking to see if they could work out just where they were on Len's map, after a minute Len pointed to a spot on the map which showed there should also be a few buildings.

There was no sign of any buildings or ruins, it was just wild woodland where nature had once again taken over.

Nothing was moving on either of the roads, so they made another mad dash. On the edge of the wood where the trees looked much more dense than the previous one they had encountered, moving on in the light of the moon, they soon came across a path which would lead them even deeper into the forest.

Again Jim volunteered to lead the way asking Len, who was at the rear, if he would try and cover up their tracks the best he could. With Tom just behind Jim taking turns cutting back an odd branch here and there when it was needed.

They had been travelling for not more than an hour, when they came across a small stream.

It was to wide for them to jump across at this point, and on either side of the stream the ground was thick with brambles, and young saplings only this narrow track would allow them to go any further, they had no choice but to enter the chilly water which was flowing quickly across it's pebbled bed.

By now, they were completely lost.

The map was of no use.

But at least they were under cover of the trees, the time was now 02:55. They decided to carry on for another hour, then if they were still in the woods would try and find somewhere to camp down and rest for a while.

Suddenly Phil cried out in pain, he had caught his leg on something in the ground. While Ken another of the machinist, bent down and, with the help of torchlight, ripped open Phil's trouser leg right up to the knee, getting a better look at the damage.

It looked really bad.

Opening a small rucksack that he had been carrying as well as his own, he said:

"Everyone, including those in the other buildings had put together a first aid kit." They all could see by the light given off by the small torches that they were carrying, that it was a bad cut about 7cm in length halfway up his lower leg. But within a few minutes Ken had cleaned and bound the wound and even put a few stitches in his trousers.

Tom, meanwhile, decided to investigate what had caused such a wound. Brushing away some rotting leaves, he discovered a piece of jagged metal buried deep into the side of the path, where the edge of the track was much deeper. He tried to dig it out, but realised that it was far too deep in the ground, but soon recognised what he was looking at was a blade of a knife of some description, probably dropped by someone many years ago.

While leaving Phil to rest for awhile, Tom and Jim decided to have a look around and check the area.

They had not gone far when Jim said "I've had the feeling that they were being watched for quite awhile now." Tom agreed, he had felt it and had heard rustling in the bushes but thought it was just a wild animal looking for food.

They both realised that they may have company, and whoever they were, they were very close.

Both agreed not to say anything to the others yet, and went back to see how Phil was doing if he was fit enough to continue.

After another 20 minutes or so marching , they came across an opening in the trees that was big enough to see the sky and rest.

They had just settled down, Jacob had just begun to sort out something to eat, when they heard someone or something approaching through the undergrowth; whatever it was it was moving fast.

Not knowing what to expect: had their escape been found out quicker than anyone had anticipated and was it them coming after them this very minute? The only weapons they had were Steve's automatic pistol with a few rounds of ammunition and Jacob's meat cleaver, which he still had strapped to his back. When a group of armed men came rushing through the bushes into the clearing, neither Steve nor Jacob had time to react.

The armed men had them surrounded.

One of the men, who seemed to be in charge, came forward and after he quickly assessed that they were not otherwise armed, asked: "Have you just escaped from the prison?"

Jim said they had, and explained why they were there. The man went over and spoke to the rest of his group, out of range of the fugitives.

Tom could not hear what had been said, but when there seemed to be some kind of a agreement between them, he returned and beckoned them to follow. Jim asked if someone could take a look at Phil's leg, one of the men who had been talking to others of his party, came over to Phil carrying a black bag. A bag just like the one that doctor had carried who came with the visitors when the man had died. All the fugitives stepped forward forming a shield to protect Phil; the man smiled and told them not worry, that he was just going to have a look.

After examining the wound, he then washed and cleaned, then said it would need some more stitches in, it is the best he could there.

He asked Phil if he was able to walk and said whoever had done the stitching had done a good job, but he would have a better look when they were back at camp.

The one that they had mistakenly taken to be in charge came over and told them to be ready to move shortly, he still had not told them who they were, or even introduced himself or any of the others.

Travelling in silence they were led along paths through some marshy ground, then crossing a small but quite fast-flowing stream.

Even though they were walking in single file, their guides kept pushing them along at breakneck speed.

No-one had said a word since starting the journey. It was Tom who decided to ask where they were being taken. Everyone stopped. Someone told him that they would be there shortly.

"By the way, my name's Charles," said the man. "You seem to have the idea that I'm in charge here. There's no need for leaders in our group. We're all equal. Maybe it was because I spoke to you first that gave you that idea."

He continued:

"And it will be the council of representatives that will decide what to do with you all, as it won't be long before those from the Work Zone, as you call it, will be hot on your trail. We'll try and divert them, as best we can, but we can't, of course, guarantee for how long."

A further thirty minutes, at a quick pace, passed, when they realised that they were crossing the same stream they had crossed earlier, but further down from where they had entered before.

Walking in the shallow waters for fifteen minutes, they came across what looked like loads of piles of old bricks and timber.

They soon realised that this was where they were being taken.

Over the whole area, there were old buildings being stripped to the ground for their materials, right down to their very foundations. Then everything would be sold so that new ones could be built.

Just away from the site, Tom could see several caravans and tents, where women and children looked on in bewilderment.

As they entered the little compound, people seemed to appear from everywhere: a mixture of all ages and colour.

Most of the men were covered in dust.

Even the children were curious about the strangers. Tom still regarded Charles as the leader, who now guided them to an area around a fire. Charles left them to get warm while he went over to speak to a woman that had been standing by a fire. After giving the newcomers a once-over, and, without saying a word, she turned and headed over to a large oven, built out of old bricks, out in the open air the fire underneath was well lit.

On top, stood a huge iron pot. They watched as the woman picked up a ladle. After stirring the contents for a few minutes, she began to fill several dishes with the thick liquid. As each bowl had been filled, a small toddler took it over to each one in turn.

Sitting on a log by the fire, Tom soon finished off his bowl. He had been much hungrier than he thought. He sat quietly, watching everyone going about their business. Even though it was still very early in the morning, it was just beginning to get light, and promised to be a nice day.

He felt a tug at his trouser leg. Looking down, he saw a little boy and girl.

Their arms were full of different cans of food. The woman with them told them that the cans were for them to take on their journey.

All the women and the children sat watching the strangers eat.

Tom would never have thought just a few weeks ago, that the only thing he knew about females, was what he had read and seen in old magazines or papers.

Now they were sitting just a few metres away.

But he still couldn't get the image or the smell of the red-headed woman out of his head.

Sitting there watching the children playing amongst the trees and in the mud, Tom began to reminisce of when he too had been little, like these children here.

But there the similarities ended.

He had never been free to wander about or to play.

They were kept locked away inside, in little groups, being taught their different trades and professions.

He felt cheated and a little jealous of these children who were playing and laughing and began to rue what he had missed.

Then Charles began to explain that most of them here were professionals or had trades like engineers, doctors etc. all sorts, who just liked being free, moving about in the open.

"That woman that served you the porridge," he said casually, "she used to be a cardiologist until she married Teddy. Then they decided to join us."

He observed the men's reactions.

"He's a painter and decorator. Do you know what I mean?"

He continued:

"To survive, we strip down all these old buildings then sell the materials. Because the materials are so scarce, there were not enough people left to produce all that's required for civilisation to survive.

"Nobody really knows or cares what happened in the past. It's gone. But some of us think differently: it may come back and bite us one day. We don't get involved in their politics, so nobody ever comes here or bothers us as long as we abide by the rules. So you see you've put us in a bit of a spot. If they ever found out or even thought that we've helped you… well, what they would do to us is anyone's guess."

Now it was Tom's turn. There was something he

was meaning to ask Charles; something that been on his mind since they'd first met. This was his chance now to question him.

"Why did you ask me, when we first met, if we were the ones that had escaped from the prison? And, what did you mean by 'prison'? How long have you known about us being locked away inside the Work Zone?" Surprised at the question, Charles said:

"We've known about the prison from way back. We've been keeping an eye on it just in case someone, like yourselves, escaped. And before we go any further, I'd like to know what crimes you've all committed."

"Crimes?" asked Tom.

"Yes. Have any of you, say, robbed or committed a felony?"

"No, we've never robbed nor killed anyone. We were only children when we were brought here. We've been there ever since. We were just boys, just like those playing here in the camp."

Charles couldn't find the words to describe just how he felt, after what he had just heard, and the significance of Tom's answer was so horrific to anyone that valued their freedom as much as they did.

Just then a woman came over carrying a jug filled with what to Jim and the others looked like dark brown water.

The woman saw the looks they were giving the liquid. She smiled.

"It's just ale," she said. Jacob, being a chef, was willing to taste almost anything, took the first sip. At first he wasn't quite sure what to make of it. He certainly hadn't tasted anything like it before.

Seeing that after the second and third sips he continued to drink till he had emptied the cup of it's contents, they quickly emptied their cups hoping for more. Charles came over with another woman, whom he introduced.

"This is Catherine we are partners, she will give you everything that you will need on your journey, then one of us will guide you till you are far enough away for our safety. I'm afraid that is all we can do, so as soon as you are ready you'll have to be on your way.

"Because it won't be long before they are on your trail, we must get you as far away from here as possible.

"You must not be found anywhere near here.

"Before you go there is something else that I would like to show you." Taking Tom by the arm he led him to a gap in the trees and pointed out over the valley to a small lake: "That's Tritiford Millpool, running alongside is the River Cole, that is what we followed earlier, do you remember?

"Following that way would lead you to a populated area, but that's the way we are going to take you, in the opposite direction, out into the open countryside. By the way we will have to get you some different clothes; the ones you are all wearing give you away."

So as soon as they had finished their refreshments and the doctor had checked Phil's leg to make sure he was able to carry on, Phil insisting that he was, so after their farewells, reluctantly, they were on their way again.

Following behind the man who had offered to be their guide, they were moving at a much faster pace than they had before, and were soon gasping for breath and asking their guide if he would slow down a little, but he still would not slow down the pace.

He told them that he would not, "not until they were far enough from the camp," which they understood, they had been going for about fifty minutes, when suddenly he stopped.

Then in front of them another stretch of water, but this was different it was more formal, it had sides that were built up vertical rather than the broken slopes of the brooks and streams.

Looking into the distance they could see some kind of gate or dam, blocking the water's flow, it also looked pretty straight compared to the streams that zigzagged through the woods which they had crossed many times today, and it was also much wider and looked much deeper.

Len, turning to their guide, asked if he knew where they were when he showed the guide his old map. Their guide pointed to a spot and he began to trace one of the thin black lines, which he explained.

"They were canals and this one," he pointed, "was the Stratford Canal.

"And they are," pointing towards whatever it was blocking the flow of water, "they are what we call lock gates. I won't explain their usage, you will not need to know how to use them.

"This way heads south from Birmingham going down to Stratford." He seemed keen to explain the whole of the canal system to them as they walked. "Further down It also leads off to join the Grand Union Canal at a place called Lapworth, from there you would be able to go all over the country. Marvellous things," he added.

Following the line backwards Len realised that it passed right by the prison. Could it be the same one he had seen from the roof many times, the one which had brought them here all those years ago?

Ken, who had come over to have a look, curious where they were, suddenly recalled the time when he too had passed this way as child, all those years ago, when he had been able to get a glimpse of the open countryside, through a hatch that had been opened a little just to let some air in the confined space.

Still walking at a fast rate the guide seemed to veer of the main path taking a path through thick woodland filled with bushes of the Buddleia, packed with red, white and dark blue flowers. Further on there were shrubs of the rhododendron and bushes of wild roses, all growing wild amongst the trees.

The wild roses that grew in abundance all along the narrow path, filling the air with a beautiful fragrance.

He kept them moving until they came across a river.

This stretch of water seemed to be travelling much faster than the last, but still quite shallow. The pebbles on the bottom and on sides of the stream looked slippery and the water cold.

Making their way along the edge of the river for a while, then their guide brought them to a sudden halt, advising them:

"Walk in the middle of the river for another twenty minutes, then come out and on your left you will see a clearing, surrounded by young saplings. It's well hidden so you will be able to take a rest.

"But not for too long." He told them that it was time for him to turn back and that he must leave them.

"We have been going south, away from the most populated areas, so now you have a good chance of missing anyone so good luck."

With that he turned and was out of sight in no time, leaving them to decide what they must do: to trust what he had said or please themselves.

They decided that they had no choice but to take his advice, because they had no idea where they were, so with the aroma of the wild flowers filling the air, they were on their way. In the middle of the river the water was freezing and their flimsy shoes were no protection against the cold and the pebbles under foot. They had not thought to bring the tough working boots, that they all worked in. But still they carried on in the direction that they had been told.

The going was hard work, the pebbles at the bottom were slippery and once in a while one of them would slip and go over. By the time they decided that they had gone far enough, it was then the clearing their guide had told them about was spotted just in front of them, it could not have come at a better time. They were all soaking wet and were glad to leave the river and walk on dry land.

After walking a further ten minutes away from the

edge of the river, they decided that it would be safe to take a rest, have something to eat, and also a chance to dry some of their clothes.

While Jacob began to prepare a meal, the rest of them hunted for dry wood to make a fire.

Mark and Phil, with the aid of a couple of thick branches that Mark had cut off a young sapling to help Phil get along better with his injured leg and could also be used as a weapon if needed, went off to explore what lay ahead.

It was still early morning, the sun had just risen over the tops of the trees and the air was getting quite warm, so by the time the rest of them had something to eat, they lay there, waiting nervously for Mark and Phil.

Phil seemed to be managing quite well with his injured leg and they waited, lying there completely naked on the dry grass, enjoying these moments of peace, just watching their clothes drying in the gentle breeze.

Soaking up the sun, just knowing to have experiences like this and the freedom to make their own decisions made it all worthwhile, yet they all knew the search would have begun, and what the final outcome would be.

But for the first time in their lives they were able to laugh out loud about it. Jim suddenly broke the silence.

"There's one thing that is in our favour and that is the dogs that once patrolled between the fences were taken away a few years back, so the guards have no means of tracking us. They'll either have to wait and send for new ones, or try and track us themselves."

After a while Phil returned with an arm full of dry wood, explaining:

"Mark's carried on following a track made by some wild animal to try and find out where we're heading and how far the wood stretches."

Jim asked: "Phil, how's your leg?"

"Not too bad," Phil said, but something in the way the answer came out gave them reason to have their doubts, that it was not as good as he made out, but no-one wanted to push it any further for now.

It was another forty minutes before they heard movement coming, but from a different path than the one that Phil had approached from, and it was heading in their direction.

Suddenly Mark broke out into the clearing.

They were all relieved to see him.

Now they could breathe again. As he sat down he said:

"I've been following the track to where the wood ends. It isn't far from here and opens out into a huge pool of water. I think it feeds the river we've just left."

"I wonder if that river could be the River Cole," Tom said.

Referring to the map, Len said:

"It could be. There's a pool here on the map just where the canal turns south, as the guide said."

"Further on, there's a path running alongside a canal. It could be the one that we'd seen earlier," Mark added.

"But here on the map there seems to be some kind of junction with another canal which diverts off," said Len, taking a reference from his map.

"It's probably the Stratford Canal which does run south according to this map, the other leads across to a place called Lapworth, which then goes off all over the country."

"I don't think we'll get that far," said Jim, with a smile.

When eventually they did reach the path that ran alongside the canal, it was the middle of the day. They had not heard anyone chasing them, but they knew that it was only a matter of time. Moving swiftly along the path, keeping well into the side of the hedge, they came to a small aqueduct crossing over a fast-flowing stream.

Moving on along the towpath for another fifteen minutes they could see in the distance what looked like some kind of frame crossing over the canal.

As they approached and they were a little closer they could see that the frame was there just to lift the bridge, when boats wanted to travel up or down the canal.

On the other side, and just a little way up the narrow lane, they could make out the skeleton of a building. The roof had fallen in many years ago and there were no doors or windows left, they had long gone to be used elsewhere, and everywhere was slowly being eaten away by nature. A sign lay on the ground, rotting with age and covered with mud, weeds and long grass growing in the dirt, making the word painted on the wooden panel hard to recognise. Joe's persistence in cleaning away the debris meant they could just make out the name, Drawbridge.

But right now, they had no time to investigate: they had to decide which way to go.

Len looked up at the sky towards the sun and decided the best way to take. No-one argued with him.

"Why have you decided to go this way?" asked Jim.

Pointing in the direction of the sun, Len replied:

"It always rises in the east and, at the moment, it's to our right."

He checked his watch.

"The time's now 13:30. so we must be heading south along the canal system but I think that we should get off the towpath for a while and cut through the woods again."

"Which way do you suggest we go?" asked Jim.

He checked the map, and ,with a finger, followed the wriggly line.

"This must be the river that we've just left," he said, "and this in blue is the canal."

Studying the map they realised that the area now covered in forest had once been a very populated area full of houses, so if they turned right through the forest it would take them away from the main populated areas, then join the canal further down.

"But with the path running alongside, we should be able to put as much distance between us as quickly as possible, and if this is where we are now it means that we must have only covered about five or six kilometres in about ten hours?" asked Tom.

"Yes," replied Jim, "but you have to take into account all the times we have stopped, and we were zigzagging all the time, and that it was not our intention to cover as much ground as possible. I thought we wanted to see as much as we could."

They checked the map again, trying to decide if it would be better to carry on south towards Stratford or east to Lapworth.

When Steve told him to lead the way, Len chose to go east, and without another word they all agreed and from then on he would be referred to as the navy.

After packing all their gear together they turned off the towpath cutting through the woods, hoping to throw those chasing them off for at least a little while. It was mid-afternoon when Len retrieved a small compass from his bag.

"If we've been going south east for the last thirty minutes," he said, "so we should be joining the canal again soon."

Reaching the canal towpath again they were able to go at a much brisker pace, and along the canal towpath they soon began to cover a lot more ground, but remembering to keep a look out for anything coming along the canal or any sounds or signs of those pursuing them.

They all realised that those back at the zone would be aware of their disappearance by now, and even if they had not found the place of exit or the direction they had taken, the whole area would soon be swarming with security.

# 5

They weren't far wrong. Back at the zone everything was in a state of panic. The governor had been in touch with central office situated Birmingham, and now those sitting in their comfortable chairs at the headquarters in Brussels had been informed of the breakout and were not too pleased.

They had spoken to Margaret Storrs who had been busy over the last two weeks looking at several more such zones, and she had been in touch with the governor, instructing him to wait for her arrival. She would be coming to take charge with Dr Caroline Pearson [everybody for some reason always referred to her as Dr Caroline]. That is where the familiarity ended because they all knew and feared the power that she possessed; could it be that she had very important family connections or the relationship she had with Margaret Storrs? Either way no one would choose to pick a fight with her.

Margaret Storrs had also notified him that she would be bringing others, some that he already knew. They had already been to the zone previously and he had made their acquaintance, but she would also be including some of her own professionals.

Ninety minutes later she arrived with Dr Caroline and twenty of her own men.

Also with her were the two doctors, John and Yvonne Dampier, who had accompanied her previously with the rest of the group; they all knew each other from the first visit.

Both John and Yvonne were experts in their fields of work as psychoanalysts.

But this would push both their expertise and strength to the limit.

And it was going to take a lot longer than any of them could have imagined. It had been a while since Johns and Yvonne's last visit to the zone, and they had been hoping that it would have been their last, but luck was not on their side. That morning they had been informed there was an emergency, and there would be transport on the way to pick both of them up, and take them directly to the zone.

That would be all they would be told till they arrived, nothing of the men that had escaped had been mentioned.

Everyone had been waiting in the governor's office for the best side of a hour, for John and Yvonne to arrive.

And they were still waiting to find out where and how the men were able to get away, without anyone hearing anything. So by the time John and Yvonne had arrived they were in a not very good mood or impressed with the standard of security.

The governor was taking full responsibility for the whole charade.

Margaret Storrs was furious, no-one dared to say a word, it would be another fifty minutes before they were told about the ventilation shafts, and that the external grill had been removed. Another thirty minutes before the route around the pig sties and the hole at the back of the chicken house had been found, and a hole leading out through the fence was to be discovered.

One of the security guards had been sent through the hole in the fence to follow the track through the undergrowth, while others went to investigate the outer perimeter fence.

So they should soon know the whereabouts of the fence where the men had exited the area.

By the time a heavily armed group had been assembled near where the exit point of the fence had been discovered, it was well past noon, with the orders that there were to be no prisoners.

"If anyone was seen to be helping these men in any way, they too must be dealt with. That comes from the very top. If any of you have any doubts about this let me assure you it does. No-one must ever know about this, nor what happens here inside the zones. Is that understood?"

All the time Margaret Storrs was making her little speech she had been watching John and Yvonne, wondering if these two could keep a secret even if they wanted to.

The two doctors just looked at each feeling quite

uneasy with what they had just heard, but at the moment there was nothing that they could say or do.

Outside the fence they had soon found the point where the men had made their escape, and with all the guards running along the edge of the forest, it didn't take them long before they found the track the escapees had used to escape into the forest.

The man given the responsibility of capturing the men was a young captain going by the name of Captain Turner.

Yvonne remembered him as the officer who had stood all alone at the first meeting who, though he still had his boyish looks, and he soon showed from the start that he would not be making things easy for any of them, including both Margaret Storrs and Dr Caroline.

This didn't go down too well at first with Margaret Storrs, but when he told them, "He was ordered not to take any nonsense from anyone. That everyone that had been here at the first meeting had marks against them with no exception," he looked at each one in turn as he spoke to them. "I have the full backing of those down at the central office and those sitting on the European committee."

No-one said a word.

Now Yvonne realised why this young captain had stood away from the table, he had been taking everything in and taking notes. This young man was another that had to be watched she thought to herself.

She felt her face flush when she realised that he had been watching her, a boyish grin spread from his mouth to his eyes as she returned the smile and he gave a little bow of his head.

"And by the way I do not like the idea that one of our own is armed with an automatic and plenty of ammunition."

They knew by the tone of his voice that he meant every word that he said. They also realised they had to take what the man said without question. So in single file, they all followed him and his guards. All they had to do now was to try and keep up with them, and just follow the path the prisoners had made. Everybody was in a joyful mood, and began to think it was going to be easy, just a day out, a walk through the woods; even Margaret Storrs and Dr Caroline were chatting away like two young schoolgirls.

Even some of the guards had began to treat it as a sport, moving along at a fast pace calling back at Yvonne and John, telling them to keep up and they would all be home for tea, but there was a look of contempt from the young captain that should have warned the others that he was thinking differently. They soon realised that this was just a small copse, and they were soon facing another wide road that at this time of morning was fairly busy with traffic.

Running along the side of the road, the place where the men had entered the second forest had been spotted fairly quickly, but now after a short distance into the trees, it soon became apparent that the captain had been right to be cautious. It was not going to be as easy as they first thought.

Without the aid of the sun's rays it had became more difficult to follow which path the fugitives had taken. They frequently came upon spots where the paths split into several different routes or where the path veered off in two directions. The young captain ordered his men to slow down to the delight of those following behind. At each junction he sent one of his men to see if there were any clues to which path the fugitives had taken, then they had to stop and wait till each one had returned safely, and were sure they had found the path the fugitives had taken.

When Margaret tripped over a branch that had been carefully concealed under some leaves, the captain told them it had probably been placed there deliberately and that they should all be very careful where they tread from now on because "Those men are not so simple as we were led to believe." He added. He gave Margaret Storrs a look that was better than a thousand words. From then on everyone kept their eyes open for anything that looked faintly suspicious across the paths or up above in the branches. Occasionally there would be something lying on the path, which would be carefully inspected before moving on. It would hinder their progress and nothing that would harm anyone was found. This had not gone unnoticed by the young captain and he told them so.

Then the path they had been travelling suddenly changed. Looking as if no-one had come this way for years, the captain realised that they had missed something along the way, where had the men had turned off?

So now they would have to backtrack all the way back till they found where they had left the path. By now they all had begun to realise that this was not going to be so easy.

The going was getting harder with every step and John and the three women began to feel the strain the most.

So when Dr Caroline suggested they should slow down the pace even more, they were surprised when the captain obliged.

It was now early evening.

The captain asked Margaret Storrs: "Do you intended to camp out here with the men or return to the governor's house tonight? If it's the latter I suggest that you shouldn't leave it too late before starting back. That's if you don't want be stuck in the forest at night."

"I think it would be better if we all went back tonight," said Storrs.

It took all the young officer's willpower to hold back a smile, he had not thought for one minute that any of this little group would cherish the thought of spending the night out here. When he thought about it, neither did he.

But he would send his sergeant and a couple of men to guide them back while he and the remaining men would look for the place where the fugitives left the path, then look for a suitable site to make camp.

When eventually they found the spot they had missed and had set up camp for the night, even the guards were exhausted.

As the sergeant took them back along the path they had just travelled a couple of hours ago, John began to think how lucky they were that the young captain and sergeant were such professionals. He hated the thought of being stuck out here without them, god knows what was out there.

How on earth were those men managing? They must be frightened with all the sounds of the evening. John could not imagine what they must be feeling. He wasn't the only one wondering along those lines.

Back at the camp, the captain could not understand how those men, who were supposed to have never been outside those buildings, were not just managing, but had started wandering around and not getting lost. It seemed as if they had spent their whole lives out here in the forest.

How is it, the young captain thought to himself, that these men were able to move about and not be seen or heard? He wondered if they had been seen and he could not help but feel a little bit of admiration for them.

After making sure that everything in the camp and the watches had been organised, and the rest of the group had been sent back to the zone a good forty minutes earlier. He decided that he would go and see if he could find the camp of those scavengers that he had been told were working this area.

He had been informed before about the scavengers: it was a name given to the groups of people that wandered around the country, looking for old ruins, where their materials could be re-used. He was told they often stripped down derelict buildings, and went about their business lawfully.

When everyone was settled down the young captain set off on his own to see if he could find them. He had been told they were working around this area, so there was a good chance that their site was near.

What he wanted to find out from them was if they had seen or heard anything of the missing escapees.

As he made his way along the muddy path he was quite happy: he didn't mind the mud or the noise of the forest and he had time to think.

It wasn't long before he realised he had company, and that his every step was being watched with interest, even if he could not see or hear them he knew they were there.

But all he could do for now was to carry on, and wait and see who they were, and what were their intentions.

Another five minutes went by and still they had not shown their faces and he had begun to think it was his mind playing tricks. When he came to a crossing, and was just deciding which path to take, something moved out of the bushes behind him. Moving swiftly, and with his instinct and training his movement was swift, he brought his pistol out of it's holster in one movement.

He knew it had been a foolish mistake. Facing him a single man stood smiling, confidence showed with his body language.

The young captain put his pistol back in its holster, stepping forward the man held out his hand in a sign of friendship to meet him.

"If you are after those men, they passed through the crossroads an hour or two ago. We kept a eye on them until the brook, by then we knew you were coming, so why are you after them?" the stranger asked, before explaining who he was.

Captain Turner knew that this man was not alone, also any sudden movement would be a mistake.

"That doesn't concern you," said the young captain, trying to press his authority on the stranger, but he might as well have saved his breath. The man just turned and, without saying a word, disappeared into the woods.

Following the stranger the young captain suddenly realised that now they had left the main path, and he had no idea in what direction they were heading.

Close to the stranger's heels the captain followed, not wanting to get lost in here, god knows how long it would take him to find his way out, because now trees and the undergrowth were getting thicker with every step.

The man in front must have sensed his concern, he had slowed his pace down enough to allow the young captain to catch up.

When he was close enough, the captain apologised for his rash remark.

With that, the stranger stopped, and said "My name is Charles."

The captain introduced himself.

"I'm Captain Turner of the security forces from London. We've got to find those men quickly, they are very dangerous."

Not realising that the man he was talking to had just recently befriended the very men he spoke about.

"By the way," Charles added, "it was not just human eyes that were watching your every movement captain."

Turner could not help thinking that the *captain* part had been said with jest, but now he was more concerned with what else might be roaming through these woods.

"What other creatures are out here?" He could not help the sound of concern from the question, he like everyone else had not thought of anything other than feral cats roaming around.

"Well for a start there are wild boar not far from here if you leave them alone you will come to no harm, then there's the packs of dogs. They ain't very nice, and the size of the cats ranging from your feral to some that had been set free from private zoos to fend for themselves, and they do, so you do not want to meet up with them."

"But don't worry too much about them, they are mostly in the southern counties of the country, but still never roam about, by yourself even if you are armed."

The young captain could not help but feel sorry for those men; they had no idea what they were walking into, but then again being shut up in those places would be no tea party either.

The more he thought about it the more he could not understood why they had chosen to escape into such a wild environment.

After a short march through the woods they broke out into a space full of people, the likes Turner had never seen before. Everyone going about their business ignoring him, even though he knew that they had seen him and the uniform that he wore.

He noticed, as they walked over to meet a group of men standing in the centre, when they had left the cover of the woods they were followed not far behind by a group of about six or seven men. Turner had the feeling that Charles would not have been alone.

Charles took him over to meet the men in the centre, who were standing away from everyone else talking.

Turner guessed that he would be the topic of their conversation.

After Charles had gone through the introductions, and a few questions where the answers were just a repeat of what he had been told before, he had the feeling that they were all hiding something and knew more than they were saying, but decided to leave it at that.

Turning to Charles he asked him if there was someone that could kindly take him back to his camp.

Led by his guide Turner made his way into the forest not taking any notice of the looks and the whispers he was getting, but he may have been concerned if he had heard the remark from one man. The man whispered into his companion's ear:

"Little does he know that we've seen many young boys enter that place, but we haven't ever seen anyone come out."

When they reached the camp, and after a quick drink and a meal, he asked the guide if he would show them the way to the brook that the man called Charles had mentioned.

The guide agreed to take them to where they had last seen the fugitives. With that the young captain instructed his men to be ready to move in ten minutes.

Fifteen minutes later they were making a quick dash through the thick undergrowth, it didn't take long before they were standing at the edge of the brook. Pointing in the direction which way the men had gone, the guide left them to their own devices.

Quickening up the pace the captain, following the path which the guide had pointed out, soon started receiving complaints from his men. They fell on deaf ears, but he soon began to spot signs they were on the right track, hoping they would soon be upon their quarry.

He was just about to stop for a rest, when one his men spotted an old stone bridge crossing over the canal further down from where they were.

Approaching the bridge, and after a quick inspection of the area, they soon realised that some of the brambles had been disturbed quite recently, hiding stone steps leading up to the bridge.

Instructing two of the men to investigate, they quickly scaled up the steep sides of the embankment and found themselves facing, on the other side of the canal across a muddy lane, a derelict building.

They slowly made their way across the bridge and when the captain and the rest of the men joined them, they decided it would be in their interest to wait there and inform Margaret Storrs what they had discovered, and their position. Watching the building for any signs of movement, they stood on the muddy lane which passed right in front of the building and waited for a reply. The two things he had noticed about this lane: one was that it had been frequently used and not too long ago either, and in the distance another property could be seen through the early evening mist; secondly the fields here seemed open and protected by well kept hedgerows, a haven for the wildlife, and the fields themselves were well cultivated and there were signs that it could be a good crop.

Their instructions were to make camp where they were, and not to approach the building, under no circumstances. They must wait until the others arrived early tomorrow morning.

As instructed they were quite happy to make camp and wait for Margaret Storrs and the others to arrive.

Now it was beginning to get dark, the night was settling in and a cold chill could be felt in the air.

Once everything had been done to make the camp secure, Captain Turner with two others went out to explore the surrounding area a bit more, keeping well away from the building.

Just a few steps more, and they would have come across another little lane running off the one on which they were standing, running parallel with the canal but on the opposite side to that they had travelled. It seemed to go down into a valley, but by now it was quite dark, the captain thought it prudent to wait, as instructed until morning to investigate further.

When eventually Margaret Storrs and the rest of them turned up around half past ten in the morning, two of the captain's men had already been sent down to investigate the lane earlier.

Wandering down the muddy path leading down into the dip, they soon heard the sound of men whispering.

Slowly working their way down the muddy slope towards the sound, they found themselves standing in front of two of the escaped prisoners: one seemed to be injured, both were cold and hungry as they had been there overnight in the freezing temperatures.

After being told what they had found, the captain instructed one of his men to have a look at the man's injuries, and that they were to be fed and kept warm. There was no objection from his men; they were prisoners and would be treated as they themselves would hope to be treated, they were professionals.

On hearing the news of the capture of the two men, Margaret Storrs was overjoyed to be able to face two of the men that had caused her so much grief in the last few days.

She had also brought with her several of her own men, they wore different uniforms than the ones worn by the captain's men, and had arrived in some kind of vehicle like a tractor-cum-people carrier, just the thing for these muddy lanes.

Looking down at the two captives, her face showed not a flicker of mercy, even before Dr Caroline could start to unpack the syringe full of the lethal dose. And before the captain could object Storrs had walked behind the two men, they had been forced down onto their knees, and as if predicting what was to come the two men held hands. Before anyone realised what was happening she had taken a pistol from one of her own men.

John realising what they were about to witness was a cold blooded execution stepped forward to protest, but he was too late: two shots rang out echoing across the valley, the bodies fell into the mud mixed with their own blood. It was too much for the young captain. He had not expected that; he had been proud of his men, and how they treated their prisoners, but this brought a nasty taste to his mouth, it would be noted.

He had been taken aback at the speed it had happened, and could only feel disdain for this Margaret Stores.

John and Yvonne could not believe what they had just witnessed, the cold- blooded killing of two harmless men who had done nothing wrong, as far as they could see.

The bodies of the two men were about put into body bags. It had been decided, while the captain and four guards would carry on down the lane, the bodies of the two men were to be sent back to the Work Zone to be disposed of in the furnace.

"Wait." It was Mark Sakes the Director of Production, it was the first time he had said a word since they had started out, not even to complain about the state of his clothes, which everybody had commented on how smart he always looked. At the start he had taken it all in good humour, as they travelled through the woods, his safari suit had become torn and dirty, his boots were like everyone else's, covered in thick mud but still he had not complained.

"Has anybody here asked themselves why were these two men had been left here, when they know we would find them, and they also know what the consequence would be?"

"One of them is injured sir." It was one of the guards that had first discovered the men.

"Where?" Sakes asked.

"The right leg, sir."

Yvonne was amazed, how tenderly Sakes cut through the material of the trouser, as if the man was still alive, and he spent a few seconds inspecting the wound.

"Have any of those men got medical experience? If not, how come this wound has been stitched professionally?"

When he stood up, the look he gave the two doctors was a warning that they weren't there for a day out but to do a job.

Even Dr Caroline was taken back.

"I think that we were too anxious in executing those two men. We may have been able to find out if anyone was helping them. Maybe that's why we aren't able to catch those fugitives."

"There's no-one round here that would dare help them," said Margaret Stores.

"There are posters everywhere saying that if anybody is found to be helping them, they would suffer the consequences." Margaret Stores was determined to have the last word.

Maybe not, the young captain thought to himself, he was thinking of the scavengers hiding in the woods.

It had been a hard first day and night for those men.

# 6

While Margaret Stores and her group of officials were busy carrying out the execution of Mark and Phil, while the sergeant, with two of his men, went off to inspect the derelict building.

They soon found evidence, in each of the rooms, that the prisoners had been there not too long ago.

Rejoining the main party, the sergeant explained what they had discovered and recommended that they should be on the move, as quickly as possible. Both the captain and Margaret, who had been listening attentively to what the sergeant had been saying, agreed, and that the sergeant, with two of his men, should go on ahead, while the captain and the rest of the men stayed with the group in case the fugitives returned.

"What about your own men?" Turner asked.

She knew what the young captain was referring to.

"Captain they are under my directive and as I have said before those men we chasing are *Beyond Salvage*, and that comes from EUROPE. Is that good enough captain?" and the two bodies can be taken back and burnt.

The sergeant, with two of his own men set off in pursuit of the fugitives. But what none of them had realised, was that their every move was being watched.

Just a few hours earlier the prisoners had travelled that very same path. Travelling along the towpath at a quick pace putting one man about fifty metres in front and one the same distance behind, so they could give a warning if anything came along the path or canal.

The embankment rose steeply, there would be nowhere to hide.

There seemed to be a lot more traffic along this stretch of water than before, and they soon realised that if they continued along this path, it would not be long before they were seen and reported.

At the next opportunity they decided they would have to exit the towpath. It was sheer luck when they came across steps, mostly hidden with brambles, nettles and knee-high grass. If it had not been for the bridge Len would never have seen the steps, cut into the side of the bank leading up to the top, where the old stone bridge crossed over the canal, five metres above them. Clearing some of the nettles and brambles away that were concealing the steps, now with a little bit of luck they would be able get off the towpath before being spotted.

Turning to Jacob, who had been walking at the rear, Jim asked:

"Could you pull some of the brambles back over, as he made his way up the steps, just enough to conceal the steps from those following?" It had been slow work and it had taken another 40 minutes before they were all standing on the bridge. They all bore the scars and stings of their labours. Eventually the last of them had reached the top and they had done the best that they could to conceal the whereabouts of the steps. Facing them on the other side of the bridge, they found themselves looking at a strange derelict building.

Curious to find out what kind of building it was and its function, and the purpose of that sign swinging gently in the warm evening breeze, a picture of a flower, nearly faded out of all recognition through age and weather.

"I think it is picture of a bluebell, which is a wild flower that grows in abundance amongst the trees," Phil said.

The building itself lay on the other side of the bridge and had been overgrown by many years of neglect with ivy, brambles and young trees, and scattered over the parts of the ground that had not yet been taken over were a few old tables with seats, but even these were being slowly taken over or rotting where they stood. All of them were reluctant to be the first to cross until Steve, the ex-guard, stepped forward, telling the others to get under cover in case this was a trap.

He made his way very slowly towards the old stone bridge, peering over the stone wall, at the stretch of water below, looking for any signs of life. Nothing moved. Not a sound could be heard. There were no signs of life. There was only the sound of the sign swinging in the breeze.

Disappearing into the distance, what in the past

would have been a narrow road was now just a muddy lane. Yet, there all around them, were signs it was still used, many deep tracks of a very large vehicle.

Trapped in between the high edges on both sides, was the lane that went off in both directions. In one direction he could just make out another house and, from its tall chimney, a wisp of smoke drifted away in the breeze, a warning that there were people about and that they must be careful.

Curious to see what lay ahead, and with each step, Steve's fingers tightened their grip around the stock of the gun ready to fire at the first signs of an ambush.

As he made his way across the bridge, looking for the slightest movement, taking no chances, keeping a eye on the building, wondering if there was still someone inside watching his approach.

Occasionally looking behind, just to make sure that the others were well hidden, not being able to see them he knew they would be safe, and deciding that he had passed the point of no return, he carried on making his way across the lane towards the building. He could feel his heart pounding.

For the first time in his life, he felt he had a purpose, still watching for any movement, clutching his automatic gun close to his side, he approached. Tightening his fingers around the trigger, he looked through into a passage that ran between two separate buildings, leading out into a grassed area. He looked down on the canal below, tables and benches lay amongst the long grass and rotting weeds, before walking slowly along the passage, hoping to find the entrance into the bigger of the two building. Both buildings were built in a reddish brick with the paint on one of the window frames having mostly disappeared years ago, and now the frames themselves were rotting away.

He was in luck. To his left, there was an opening. Giving the door a slight push, it fell off its hinges, crashing to the floor, sending pieces of glass all over the place. The noise was horrific.

What those waiting on the other side of the bridge must have thought, Steve could only wonder.

Stepping over the broken door and the broken glass, Steve brushed aside the broken glass the best he could with his feet. When he thought he had done enough he carried on through the rooms.

Moving quietly inwards, taking his time, Steve stepped slowly into a large area where a few tables and chairs had been pushed away in a hurry. They were scattered around and were now covered in a fine layer of dust, and broken glasses lay around the floor.

Moving silently through the rooms, one by one, listening for anything that would warn him of any trouble ahead, stopping now and then to study some of the photos that covered most of the walls.

But there was nothing, just the smell of dampness and dust, but now and again there was the sound of a window being slammed shut by the wind. Steve stopped and waited a few seconds studying the coating of dust that covered the floor. It indicated that no-one had crossed this way for a very long time.

Deciding that it would be OK to call the others, then they could cover all the rooms in a very short time and see if there was anything that might be of use.

Even now that he knew that there was nobody in the building, every time one of the windows slammed shut he jumped expecting someone to be there, and he didn't feel any better when the others arrived.

Now he thought at least he would have help, but it didn't help especially when he realised that Tom had been standing beside him without him even hearing him creep up.

"This place gives me the creeps," said Steve. "And what kind of place do you think it had been all that time ago? It looks as if no-one's been here for years. And what's that horrible smell? It seems to linger in all of the lower rooms. Have you seen the floor?

"It's littered with broken glasses and bottles. Did they never think of clearing up before they left?"

Tom just shook his head in amazement. Why was Steve so concerned about the condition this place had been left?

It was then Ken, who had been looking around the lower floors, came up with the answer. Picking one of the broken bottles up off the floor, he pointed to its label and told them that they called these places public houses; where people met socially for drinks.

"That's the hops you can smell," he said, "don't you remember back at that camp the drink they gave us? It's the same drink and that's what you can still smell even after all these years. It must've been quite strong stuff."

"How do you know all this?" asked Steve, realising that it was a silly question because he knew that he would never get the answer; they never asked each other where they got certain information from.

He would never find out about the secret tit bits of information that everyone kept either, and where did Ken get that old map that he kept in his pocket? Steve knew that he would never know, nor did he expect to. Ken just winked. Looking out of one of the windows, Tom stood in silence, thinking: where had everyone gone and what had happened to them? Jim, who had come up to the second floor with the rest, stepped up alongside Tom and asked:

"How could so many people just disappear?"

It had been something they all had been thinking about for quite a while now. Looking at the pictures hanging on the walls in every room, Leo, thinking aloud, asked:

"Why didn't they bother taking the pictures with them?"

After returning from a stint around the outer buildings and having missed most of what had been said, Jacob came over to see what all the fuss was about. Then, like the rest, a look of bewilderment crossed his face as he looked around at the pictures on the wall, he could see the place had been empty for years.

"Another thing, how many people have we seen other than the scavengers?" Leo asked.

"I could count on my one hand just a few boats going up and down the canal, that's all."

"He's right," Joe said. "If we had not received help from those at the camp how far do any of us think we would have got? And looking around this place I feel something is not quite right, and the sooner we are out of here the better I will feel."

Making their way down to the ground floor, they were heading for the exit when they realised that Jacob was missing.

Ken said that "he was probably wandering around upstairs," and he would go and see where he was.

He found Jacob upstairs talking to himself while he stood studying one of the pictures. It was a picture of a group of men sitting down in two rows. One of them was holding a huge shield covered with lots of miniature shields. He was a little older than the rest and his skin was darker, the same as his own; they all seemed so happy.

Jacob brushed the glass off the picture with his hand; he felt a sadness as a few tears began to run slowly over his cheeks.

Realising that Ken had left him while he had been studying the picture, he decided to go and see where he was. Hearing the creaking of the floorboards above, he decided to risk the steps leading up to the third floor. He found him in one of the small rooms, just staring into a small cupboard. The doors hung at a peculiar angle, being held in place with one single hinge.

Standing infront of the cupboard, both of them stood staring at a very old photo of a crowd of people of all ages, sitting at a large table eating and drinking, looking as if they were all having a good time in a garden which they recognised as the one with all the tables and benches just outside. The canal could just be made out in the background with lines of those narrow boats tied up along the bank. The sun was shining and everyone looked happy.

Before returning down the stairs Ken said that he would just have a look around the rest of the rooms on this floor. He waited until he heard Jacob's footsteps as he returned downstairs, before he continued inspecting the first room. Walking into one room, it was small with just one little window, the walls were covered with some kind of funny caricatures, bringing back memories. Memories of one huge nursery where the walls were full of such pictures. This must be a child's room he thought as he walked over to the window which looked out over the gardens and the canal. Then he noticed in the far corner a single child's bed frame, and as he turned to leave he kicked something lying on the floor.

Curious what he had kicked, he bent down to pick it up and looked at the object with suspicion. It had slid under the bed a little further, so he could not quite make out what it was, bending down so that he could reach under and retrieve whatever it was.

Holding it close to his face, he recognised what he had found was a child's little teddy bear: one of its legs had been half eaten by rodents, the straw filling had mostly been pulled out and one of its eyes had been lost. Holding the teddy bear close, he could imagine himself like the little boy or girl playing happy with the little teddy. Then the feeling of all those years lost as a child was overwhelming.

"What had we done?"

Rushing down the stairs to show the others what he had found, none had ever seen anything like it before, only in pictures in books that they had found. Each took a turn in holding it for a while before Ken put it safely away inside his bag. But right now they had to get moving again, before those pursuing them would be on their trail, so there was no time to hang around here for too long.

Soon they would have to start thinking of somewhere to rest for the night. It had been a long day.

"It's time to go," Joe said. "I think I noticed there was a very muddy lane or path that could have been a narrow road, when this building was a popular place. It was just as we had crossed over the bridge, across this lane."

Maybe it had been a road once, now it was just looked like a mire, overgrown with all kinds of wild plants. It would be like going into a boggy jungle, but they found to their surprise the tarmac underfoot seemed sound.

The bushes and trees had taken it over long ago, and as it ran alongside the canal, there was a section where the brickwork had been disturbed by the roots of the trees, allowing some water from the canal to flow down into the shallow hollow.

With the towpath being on the other side of the canal, they would be hidden out of sight from their pursuers, as the little group started to descend down the slippery slope, their first calamity overtook them.

Phil slipped on some wet and rotting leaves, falling into a pool of dirty water, but the fall had opened his old wound and blood started to run from the wound. Moving slightly up onto drier ground, Leo was soon ripping open the trouser leg once again, so the damage could be examined, to see how bad Phil's injury was.

There they saw the amount of blood leaking through the dressing and running onto the ground, before being congealed with the foul-smelling water of the mire.

The fall had ripped open the stitches that the doctor at the camp had closed. Now it was deep and right down to the bone and about seventy millimetres long. Try as they may to stop the bleeding completely, it was impossible. They all knew it was bad.

Phil realised that he wouldn't be able to go any further. He would only be a liability to them.

Refusing the offers to be carried further, he asked them to leave him there. He would be found by the guards. It was the mention of the guards that the others were worried about. It was only when Mark said that he would stay with him that they agreed to carry on, but Tom still had his doubts because of what would happen when those chasing them caught up with them.

They knew it would be impossible to stay and wait. After stemming the blood flow and ensuring that both understood what the repercussions might be, then and only then would they be left.

But at least they had got Phil and Mark up onto drier ground.

It had been damp in the hollow and had stunk to

high heaven. So when they reached the top, the going was much easier, and they made good progress.

A little further they had come across another ruin to their right, where most of the walls had collapsed a long time ago. They could still see the layout of the rooms but there was no time to stop and gaze with thoughts of what might have been.

Not having travelled more than a kilometre after leaving two of their comrades to the mercy of their pursuers, Tom told the others to carry on. He wanted to see if he was able see how Mark and Phil were doing, taking out the home-made telescope to start scanning back at the two companions, while the others went ahead.

"Don't be long, will you Tom?" Jacob said, as they left another of their companions.

Still making sure that he was well hidden, with the aid of the battered telescope he was able to look across the other side of the canal where he saw some movement of men in uniform creeping along the pathway leading in the direction of the two men.

Lying down on the dry grass so that he could watch without being seen, Tom could see six of the guards creeping along the bridge. But it was not the men themselves that he was interested in, rather what they were wearing. He had often seen the prison guards in their body armour, and armed, but these were somehow different.

His thoughts went back to the two men down there just chatting away, waiting for their pursuers to arrive.

Tom could not get over how relaxed both men seemed from where he was.

Now just a few metres away, the guards were setting up camp for the night. They were in no rush, even if they must have heard or seen the men sitting there.

He felt someone come and sit beside him. He realised that it was Jim who had decided to come back and join him.

Seeing that the guards were making camp, Jim told Tom the others were doing likewise, and that he might as well come and get something to eat and rest because tomorrow was going to be another hard day.

Back at camp while they ate their meal that Jacob had rustled up, they talked about their first day on the run. Realising just how tired they were, some began to turn in for the night out in the open, the first time they had ever slept under the stars, grateful that it was not raining. Strangely enough they all had a good night's sleep, with the knowledge that those chasing them were sleeping as well.

Waking up very early next morning, Jim and Tom said that they would come a little further with them, then they would like to go back and see how Mark and Phil were doing.

After an hour's walking Ken, who had taken the lead, stopped. They had come to another road crossing, and just further on an old barn.

"We'll give you three hours. One to get there, one to get back. That gives you an hour to see how Mark and Phil are. We hope they're alright."

"Where will you be heading if you aren't here?" asked Jim.

Taking out the old map, Ken pointed to a spot along a pencilled line.

"That's where we're heading, so all you have to do is follow that hedgerow. OK? Three hours, don't forget."

"Be careful. We don't want to lose anyone else," added Steve.

With that the two men were running, following along the tracks they had just come along.

They soon found the spot where Tom had sat, and with the telescope they could see the guards' camp, both watched as two of the guards reached the two men offering them food and drink, helping the injured man. Bringing them back up to their camp, one of the guards bent down and began to treat Phil's injury.

They were waiting for the other five to arrive, but when they did things changed. No sooner had she arrived, three of the party stood back, wishing to have no part of what was about to happen.

(To remain silent gives consent and to give consent gives agreement). She and Dr Caroline stood over their prisoners. What happened next neither Tom nor Jim could believe. They had just witnessed Storrs speaking to one of the armed men, who had handed her his pistol. Two shots then rang out across the open space, confirming the men's worst fears. While Storrs hovered over the bodies, Dr Caroline checked to make sure they were both dead. They were soon joined by others.

One of the men and the woman seemed to disagree

with what had just happened, but just as it looked like there would be an argument, one of the guards called over indicating that he had picked up the trail again. Now with something else to take the heat off things, again they moved off following their trail.

What they didn't realise, though, was that the whole scene had been witnessed by the very people who they were chasing.

Tom felt something inside which he had never felt before, and it did not feel right, because right now he would not be able to control himself if he could get hold of that woman or any of the bunch.

He now realised that there was to be no quarter between the two groups, and that there would no future for any of them.

He had known it from the time they had stepped into the ventilation shaft that there would be no going back, but to kill like that, without any cause; he could feel the anger building up.

Slowly he took his last look where his friends as they were put into bags and thrown into the van, but now it was time to go. He had forgot Jim was there, now both of them knew that it would be them or those down in the valley, the two men had been shown no mercy.

Running as quickly as they could to re-join the others to tell them all what they had seen.

They were soon back at the barn where the others were just finishing their meal. It had only taken just under two hours.

After hearing what Jim had told them, the rest of the group were livid.

Steve picked up his gun and was ready to go back.

If Joe hadn't restrained him, he would have gone back to meet those murderers and make some of them pay.

Instead, it was decided to get moving. It would be they that would pick the time and place, but they would pay.

# 7

Moving swiftly on, they soon came across another road junction and when they looked closer, it looked as if it was still frequently used. Turning left and moving swiftly along the hedge by the road, slipping through any gaps in the hedge they came across to avoid being seen by anyone coming along the road.

Once they came upon a narrow track made by some wild animal, and decided to follow it, cutting away any branches that blocked their way. Now the going was getting harder and they were all worn out; it had been a long day.

By the time Tom and Jim had returned after going to check on Phil and Mark and having something to eat, it was well into the afternoon. "We're in for a rough night. We'd better start looking for cover? before the rain starts," said Leo, looking up at the sky.

It was when they were looking for somewhere to rest for the night that luck was on their side. In the distance, they could just make out another building, and if they kept going the way they were they would have to pass right by it.

Approaching slowly, keeping an eye on the building for any sign of life, each one kept a look out for any movement at the windows.

It seemed that this too had been left empty, with one of the windows on the ground floor left wide open, and the floor inside covered with dry leaves. No-one was home nor had been for a very long time.

Joe quickly climbed through the open window and disappeared into the darkness, two minutes later appearing at the door.

They had found somewhere dry. while Jacob started to prepare a meal; Mike, one of the machinists, began gathered some dry leaves and an old broken wooden chair, and soon had a roaring fire going in the hearth. The others, meanwhile, went around the house, gathering all the dry leaves and wood that they could find.

Inside the derelict house the escapees were warm and happy. They had managed to elude being caught for nearly two days, much longer than any of them expected.

Their only regret was the loss of Mark and Phil.

With a blazing fire in the hearth and with a good meal inside them, they were all soon fast asleep.

The storm that Leo said would come had passed them by, but throughout the night they heard the rumble of thunder, not too far away. Every now and then the room was illuminated by a flash of lightning.

Next morning after a good night's sleep they were soon on their way, leaving the comfort of the old house as quickly as they could, they had no idea where their pursuers were, or how far behind they were.

After awhile they came across a slight incline in the narrow lane that they had been following for the last forty minutes; then they came across a small stream blocking their way.

While they were debating whether to try and wade across, or climb up the steep bank, they realised the source of the water seemed to be running down the side of the bank.

Cutting their way through thick undergrowth they slowly made their way up to the top. There they could see where all the water was coming from. Two large lakes separated by a narrow roadway, with the water lapping right up to the brim, in places over spilling the sides and down the embankment, cutting a channel into the soft soil. Over the decades it had been running; what had once begun as just a little trickle now had turned into a quick-flowing stream.

Slowly, but not sure where they were going, they began to cross. In places, the road had crumbled away and the water ran out over the side of the bank. Further on it had crumbled away completely, but someone had laid a plank of wood across the gap, so they were able to get across without getting too wet.

It was then they realised that the narrow road either went straight ahead, leading them towards a line of small properties, or went off to their left taking them between the lakes. Deciding it would be best if they stayed away from the houses, so with the water washing around their feet they headed off across the lakes; their progress was slow taking them further away from where they had left their companions.

Several times they would stop and admire all the different species of wildfowl, birds and the fish that swam about in the clear water. There were signs that wild boar had gathered here around the water's edge, yet none of the creatures seemed too concerned with their sudden appearance. Eventually, after negotiating their journey across the walkway, they were happy to be back on dry ground.

They had not enjoyed having water splashing about on either side of them, and in some places it was up to their ankles, neither did they find the thought of falling into the icy cold water too appealing, they had never seen so much water and none of them could swim.

Now they were out in open flat country, they could make out some cattle and sheep in the distance, grazing in the fields, and other fields were full of different types of crops ripening in the afternoon sun.

In the distance, they could see people working. They had enjoyed the journey, even though they had lost two of their friends. The day was getting on, and by now they were all getting tired. Overhead, clouds had gathered. The men had to find somewhere to camp for the night, and quickly too if they didn't want to be out in the open air with a storm looming. They had been on the move since dawn of the second day, and now the wind had started to pick up and there was a slight drizzle in the air, but the group's spirits were still high as they kept moving. The going was now much easier.

They had no idea how far they had travelled since escaping out of the zone. They looked back. There had been no sign of the pursuers since the execution of Mark and Phil. Maybe they too had given up for the night. Anyway, the men had a head start.

Keeping to the hedgerows most of the time, only daring to cross open fields when there was no other way, making sure there was no-one around to report their whereabouts.

They continued for another two hours, taking short rest breaks, now and then they would come upon a small copse of trees with a good view of the track they had been travelling along. Looking for the best spot to camp for the night, they checked that the ground would be dry enough to lay on.

Joe and Leo went in search of firewood while Jacob who had taken over as cook, began to prepare the food; the others checked the bags to make sure that nothing had got wet when they were crossing those lakes. Going through the two bags that Mark and Phil had given them they found eggs, fruit and vegetables. For the time being, at least, food was the least of their worries.

It wasn't long before Joe returned. He had gone on ahead of Leo, having wanted to explore the area and make sure that they were not being trapped, telling them that it was all clear as far as he could see, and that he had come across what looked like an old hut on the side of the canal.

It looked as if it could be dryer (looking up at the sky) than being caught out there in the open.

Following him through a flat shrubby area, leading away from the path that they had been taking, Tom asked:

"What direction are we going in?"

"East," said Joe. "By leaving the path, it'll make finding us more difficult. By the way, have any of you noticed that as soon as we pass, through the shrubs, they spring back, concealing where we've just been?"

No-one replied.

Just as they were beginning to wonder where Joe was taking them, they saw, amongst the hedgerow and hidden by the over hanging branches, a small hut completely covered in bramble, and loaded with ripening fruit.

The interior was dry, even though the door had fell off its hinges. They had somewhere to stay for the night.

Leo stood in the doorway, a big grin all over his face. He was carrying the body of a huge dead fowl.

"What have you got there?" asked Steve.

"It's a goose," replied Jacob. Gathering all the bags together, they all trooped inside after Joe. They were soon rewarded because what he had found was a little hut with a good sound roof and it didn't take Tom and Jim long to fix the door.

Jacob gathered the food together after he had seen to the goose, and gave Ken the job of plucking the goose. No-one asked where he had got it from.

When he had finished, Jacob showed him how to clean the insides out.

To everyone's surprise, he didn't object.

Joe was outside gathering armfuls of dry leaves together so they would have something to sleep on. There was plenty of room for them all. Once they had settled down, Jacob began to prepare some food. Soon, the hut was filled with the smell of goose roasting over the open fire.

Len went out to find some fresh water, whilst the others searched for more firewood.

"I'm just going out for a while," said Steve. "Just to see how far behind those people are. I won't be too long. No longer than an hour."

The rest went on searching for firewood, knowing that Steve would be OK.

He was the biggest and fittest of them all, plus he was armed, so if they heard any shots, they'd know that they had to get moving fast.

Jacob was left cooking the meal. It was getting late and beginning to feel a little chilly outside. Even though the clouds had begun to fill in the sky, there was a beautiful sunset.

They were all a little dispirited, often thinking of the loss of Mark and Phil.

A hour passed, and they still hadn't heard anything of Steve.

They were getting worried.

So when Jacob said that meal would soon be ready, and the smell of the goose cooking in the little hut it went a little way to cheering them. They were just about to start eating when Steve came rushing through the shrubbery: his automatic slung over his shoulder. In his hands, he was carrying a dead chicken and a container with a dozen eggs inside. All together they asked:

"Where the hell did you get them from?"

Steve smiled. He was very pleased with himself.

"I went back to where we'd seen the people working in the fields," replied Steve. "It's an open-range chicken farm. There's hundreds just walking about. Well, there's one less now, and the eggs I took one from each hatch, nobody would notice. I thought that if Jacob could cook it while he's got all his stuff out, we could have cold chicken while we're on the move tomorrow? What do you think?"

"Brilliant" said Jim.

"You didn't shoot it, then?" asked Ken, jokingly. They all saw the funny side of the question and laughed.

"Did you see anybody?" Jim asked. "But, more to the point, did anyone see you?"

"I don't think so," replied Steve. "There was no-one around."

"Then that's good thinking, Steve."

The hut began to warm-up. After their meal, they settled down on beds made of leaves, and soon fell asleep with full stomachs.

It had been another long hard day, their third on the run. They hadn't realised just how hungry they had been.

But before they could settle down, watches had to be arranged. Jacob had been excused because he was in

107

charge of the meals. Steve had the job of doing the roster to make it fair for them all.

It was Len who had been drawn to do the first hour. After another warm drink, he went out to keep watch.

Around midnight, he felt the first drops of rain. Soon, it had turned into a gale and everything outside became drenched. By the time he had been relieved of his duty, he was cold but dry. Inside the hut, it was still quite warm.

Handing the old waterproof coat that they had found hanging on a door upstairs to Jim, who was about the same size, and had been given the next hour to keep a look out. Jim would be grateful for it when he saw the weather outside the hut. It helped to keep his clothes dry.

As soon as he lay on his bed of leaves, Len allowed himself a little smile, realising they had done far better than any of them had thought they would. Now into their third day, he knew Mark and Phil would think it worth it to be free even for a little while.

With that, he allowed himself to fall into a deep sleep. While they were warm and snug in their hut, their pursuers had decided to go back to the prison again, where they could freshen up, have a change of clothes and plan what their next move would be. A dinner had been arranged in the dining room at the governor's house.

The three women had been given their own sleeping quarters; the three men were to sleep in the security officers' dormitory.

After the dinner, they all moved into a large room where drinks were handed out and the table cleared.

Mark Sykes, the area's Director of Production, was a little, overweight man.

His skin was a light brown but his eyes were the darkest John had ever seen.

He gazed at each person in turn.

"There's a few things puzzling me," he said, relaxing in a huge leather chair. "For a start," he said, looking directly at the governor, "if these men had never been in the presence of a woman or even seen one before, how do we account for the fact that when we first came here, a few weeks ago, the one person that took their interest was Dr Caroline?" He paused, just to get his breath, before continuing:

"Taking nothing from our other two charming ladies, but I noticed that it wasn't just her perfume that interested them. And if, as I myself mistakenly first thought, that they were just machines that talked, how on earth did they manage not only to escape from a secure area, but also to keep one step ahead of us? Not for one but two whole days."

"What are you saying?" asked the governor.

He sounded unhappy, thinking that he'd been accused of something. It wasn't what Sykes had said but, rather, how he had looked at him and the manner in which he'd been spoken to, that annoyed the governor so much.

"I'm just saying these men are wiser than we've given them credit for. And that, my friends, is a fact which we must accept."

The little man had them now and he knew it.

"Don't you think that they're just fighting to survive?" replied the governor.

"We mustn't forget that these men have been locked away for the whole of their lives. They know nothing about the outside world or about hate, love and ambition. My main concern is: how will they react when they realise that two of their companions have been executed. What then?"

Now it had been Yvonne's turn to make everyone aware of the consequences of their actions, whatever they may be.

Storrs seemed uncomfortable at what Sykes and Yvonne were suggesting, and went to each of the others in turn asking if any of them had any better suggestions as to the best way to handle it without attracting too much attention from the general public.

She took notes of any idea that sounded good. After a while she said that it was time to get an early night, but as they all made to move off to their rooms, it was Sykes who suggested that he and John had another look around the building again. Storrs turned to John asking him if he agreed. John said he wouldn't mind having another look inside the building.

So Storrs and Dr Caroline retired to their rooms. Yvonne stayed where she was. There was a look of concern on her face. John, realising her concern, soon put her at ease, explaining that he also wanted to have a good look around, so she too left the room.

Leaving only the four men, Captain Turner had also returned with them tonight. He had an idea which he would like to put to the other men when he had the chance, but after a few minutes he took his leave, with the governor also following. They made for the door where the captain stopped and sat down again, letting the governor leave alone.

As soon as the governor had gone, Sykes got up from his chair, asking John if he was ready to go, not even bothering to ask the young captain if he would like to join them.

John looked towards the young captain to see what his response would be. He had been totally ignored by Sykes. To John's surprise, the captain just sat there taking no notice of proceedings. There was no sign of annoyance on his face; his eyes, though, told another story.

But this young man wasn't a fool, and Sykes would be wise to remember that. He might need to turn to this young man's professionalism to get them all back in one piece.

John's thoughts were going wild.

As they made to leave, the captain gave John a wink, as if telling him not to worry so much.

Making their way across to the building, they found a guard waiting for them. They entered by the same door as before and were led into an area where crates of castings had been sorted, ready to be sent to whatever machine had been allocated the job.

The place was in total darkness. It was getting late. Most of the men that worked there would have finished for the day.

As the guard led them between the crates, he shone his torch over the incoming and outgoing castings.

"This is just the place I wanted to see," Sykes said, answering John's puzzled look when he hadn't followed the guard towards the lift. John realised that this man had no intention of going anywhere else. There was more to Sykes than met the eye.

"Let me explain," Sykes said. "A few months ago I was at a place not much different to this. By chance I found out that, over the years, they'd been using old papers and books for packing some of the more important items. The papers and books had been confiscated long back. We went through the building with a fine tooth comb, but found nothing. I still think that those men didn't let some of those papers be burnt."

Half an hour went by and they still had not found anything and were about to leave when the guards light ran across the floor and right in the corner of the area it caught something trapped under one of the crates. Swiftly the guard moved over and picked it up.

John had to hold back from laughing at the look on Sykes' face, when he realised that it was nothing other than a piece from a old order form. Wondering what Sykes had expected to find and, as if answering John's thoughts, Sykes said: "It could have been the answer to where these men were getting the knowledge from, because I've seen some interesting papers that have been used as packing before now."

"But no such papers have been found in any of the baskets here or anywhere," said John.

"I agree there's no evidence of anything that could be used as information, so is it possible, do you think, that they are just being very lucky, or are they getting a little help from people outside of the normal society like the group our young captain met yesterday?" answered Sykes.

"But I still cannot understand what was the point of killing those men," John said. He could feel his anger building up at the thought of it.

Maybe there was no other way, the man was injured and if we took him back to the zone and cared for him, what would the rest of them think.?" There was a tone in Sykes voice warning John that he had no chance of winning this argument. So John thought that it would be wise to stay silent. Looking over he could see Sykes was talking to the guard.

He could not make out what it was they were talking about, all that he knew was that this was another man that he had to be aware of and could be a danger to himself and to Yvonne.

# 8

Throughout the night a gale trashed the entire area with trees bent over with the force of the wind.

The rain rattled against the hut's windows as the men inside wondered what earth was going on.

The noise was deafening, they had never heard anything like it before, tucked away in their warm dormitories.

They feared the hut, with them in it, was going to be blown away, as it rattled and shook.

But even though the rain dashed against the windows, they were dry. The hut had done its job.

By dawn the storm had passed, the sun shone, everything looked so much different.

But in the distance, the forbidding dark clouds could be seen, warning them of more rain later.

After having had a good night's rest, they were all raring to go. They packed their bags and were soon on their way.

Before long, they came to another road. The surface was cracked and broken up by trees – both young and old – with grass and weeds sprouting everywhere.

They could see that the only vehicles that could have travelled along here for a very long time would have been tractors or farm machinery.

Following the road they found at least they could easily cover their tracks. In the morning sun, they began to make steady progress.

After walking for another hour, they came to a junction where two roads joined and twisted round a bend, they could see a few houses all in a row backing on to the side of the canal. In a couple of the gardens clothes were fluttering on a line in the sun.

On the other side of the canal working narrowboats were tied up alongside a jetty. The little group watched their crews as they sat eating, some could be seen walking up to a small building a few paces up a slight slope, fetching their drinks and meals, a few people sat at tables set outside in the gardens enjoying the sun.

"I think that could be a public house," said Len, pointing towards the small building.

Not far away a stone bridge crossed the canal carrying another highway. But this one was different, it was in good condition and had been frequently used, so keeping well hidden they watched and waited for a break in the flow of traffic.

To their left they could see the small bridge.

Maybe this was the direction they should take.

Just over the bridge, on the opposite side of the highway, they could just make out a gap in the hedge. They hoped that it would lead them on to another path.

Just in a matter of a few hours, the group had grown accustomed to travelling along these paths, even though their boots and clothes were caked in wet mud.

This path, just like the paths they had been travelling down before, looked just as overgrown, wet and muddy.

They had no idea where it would lead them, but it would get them off the highway and further away from their pursuers.

Turning to Tom, with a look of amazement on his face, Jim asked:

"I wonder where they are? We've not heard anything of them since they killed Phil and Mark. I wonder what are they planning?"

It was only when they were all across, and were well hidden out of site from any vehicles or anything coming along, that they realised that the bridge that they had just crossed went over the same canal as before. They had been criss-crossing over the same rivers and canals since they had start.

"Is this the same canal?" Joe asked, pointing towards the path.

"And I wonder where that leads to?"

All the others knew what he was referring to.

Joe continued: "The canal and that lane seem to be going in the same direction."

Again, the going was beginning to get harder. The surface had been made sodden by last night's rain, but where it was dry, it was hard and cracked.

Every few metres their way was blocked by bushes

and trees – which made it nearly impossible to get through.

After a kilometre or so, they came upon what at first looked like a huge wooden gate spanning the whole breadth of the canal – blocking any flow of water. A few metres further there was another gate, similar to the first, between them.

The water was much shallower.

Seeing the bewilderment on their faces, Ken explained: "Do you remember that guide telling us that these things are called locks?

"They enable narrowboats that we saw to travel along the canals going up and down different levels of ground. If it weren't for these, the water would flow just like a river.

"In some places there'd be pools or lakes in order to keep the canals at a certain level.

"No doubt we'll see plenty more of these on our way."

They were just about to stop and rest when Joe, who had been walking up ahead, came running back telling them that something was coming along, and travelling this way. It was then they noticed that the water was also lower on one side than the other.

But it was no time to sit and wonder, it was time to hide.

Well hidden, out of site by a huge rhododendron bush, from view of any one coming along the towpath or on the canal.

When they were satisfied that they would not be

seen, and were just about to relax, they heard a strange noise coming from somewhere ahead, the cause of the noise was hidden by the bend in the canal.

But when the contraption came into view, it took all of them back to when they had first been brought here all those years ago, probably along these same waters.

They knew what it was, and its purpose.

It was the man sitting on the roof of the cabin who they were all watching, and the way he held the gun: casually across his lap, while keeping a eye on anything that moved.

He was looking for them, and there would probably be others in the cabin below.

In silence they watched as the barge came closer not daring to move.

As the barge slowed down and stopped opposite them, the man standing in the stern guided it into the narrow entrance of the lock.

Others came out from below to handle the lock gates.

Suddenly there was movement just to the right of them, attracting the attention of the men on the barge.

Swinging round the lookout pointed the weapon in their direction, just one burst from his gun and he would have killed them all.

But while they were thinking that this was the end, a young rabbit scurried from out from under the bushes; when the soldier saw the rabbit hopping along the towpath all those on board laughed and went back to working the gates.

The man on top relaxed and carried on scanning the towpath ahead and lowering his gun.

While the whole group let out a sigh of relief, and for the moment the danger had passed.

They stayed where they were for a long time after the barge had passed through the lock and was well out of sight, too frightened to move.

Eventually Jim said it was about time they made a move, they still didn't know how far behind the others were.

They had not travelled far along the towpath when they came across another path leading off towards another stone bridge, high enough above the canal to allow the boats to travel underneath, but they could not understand the significance of the gap between both sides.

Leading off in a totally different direction, across a wild piece of ground, overgrown with nettles and brambles far worse than any of the other paths or fields they had come across.

Steve soon set too with Jacob's cleaver. He had taken on the job of clearing a path for them since entering the path, no-one complained as it was hard work and he was the fittest and seemed to enjoy the exercise so no-one bothered him.

He told the others to stay where they were while he had a look around. He had only gone a short distance when he came across a wooden gate blocking the way, but with one heave the gate crashed to the ground, both posts had, over time, rotted through.

The gateway opened out on to a field where the crops were waist high. He could see where a fox or some other wild animals had made a track through the crop.

There was no time to ponder.

It was time to get away from the waterways, they could be easily found, so making his way down to join the others and told them what he had seen and that he thought that they should get away from the canals for a while.

"Why have you taken us away from the canal towpath?" Tom asked Steve.

"I'm trying to throw them off our track for a while, hoping that they will not see the broken gate. I've covered it up the best I can and our tracks, and I think if we crossed over one of those fields in a different direction it just might give us some time, enough to see some of this land besides the canals."

The decision was taken to cross the field, but out here in the open they felt they were exposed, so just in case those chasing them found the gate, they would keep an eye out for a place where they could exit without having to chop half the trees down.

Mike had been sent ahead, while the rest of them had set up camp on the edge of the field well out of sight of anyone, making a fire for Jacob to cook a meal. It was late afternoon and they had not eaten anything since starting out that morning. They had no idea how far they had come since escaping. Mike returning was a sight for sore eyes. He had not been seen since the encounter with the barge, They were all feeling low, even with sun blazing down, and they had began to think what was the point, everything was all the same.

Mike could see that something was wrong as he approached.

"What's up?" he asked, and before anyone could answer he carried on to say:

"There's a field just ahead and we can easily get to it without having to cut away too many weeds."

After he had something to eat and drink, they were soon on the move again hoping to put as much distance between them and their pursuers as they could.

Jim broke the silence.

"I think the reason why we have not heard or seen them is because I don't think they are chasing us. All they have done is put a ring around us."

He had been quiet the last couple of hours, thinking about their situation.

"Have you noticed how everything looks the same? It's probably because we've been zigzagging along the canal system: one minute going south, the next east, then back north, covering the same old ground. If we do that, we should be safe. If we carry on, though, we'll learn nothing. All in all, I think we should take a risk and go along the canal for a while."

"I agree, but they'll slowly begin to close in on us, or just wait for us to fall into the trap," said Steve, nodding in agreement.

Keeping to the edge of a small cultivated field as much as they could, this one not as large as the one they had passed before, at the far end an assortment of small trees could be seen.

But now the going proved to be getting much harder than they had thought. To make things worse, it had started to rain again.

They forced themselves to keep going. Puddles started to gather in the troughs of the ploughed field – making it heavy going.

It was decided to start looking for somewhere to make camp for the night. Fifteen minutes later, they were still looking. The sun was still hidden behind the gathering clouds. The light was beginning to fade. The ground beneath their feet was wet and heavy and took its toll with every step. It had been well- cultivated so someone must live nearby.

Still keeping to the edge of the field, they saw, in the distance, despite the pouring rain, more figures busy at work. Inquisitive as to what they were doing, the group moved a little closer, making sure that they were well-hidden and couldn't be seen.

The light was fading fast. Their priority was to find a dry spot for the night. Luck was on their side as they soon found the remains of a small stable, meant to protect horses and cattle from the vagaries of the weather. It was open to the weather on one side, but would keep them dry for the night. Now they could relax and eat the last of the remaining food, saving just enough for the morning. Overnight the weather had improved, the rain had passed over and by early morning the sun was shining.

# 9

They were woken early by the sound of a cockerel not too far in the distance. They were reminded they were out of food after eating the last of their supplies, and on this, their fourth day on the run, their main priority was to find something to eat.

It was a beautiful morning, the sun wasn't too warm yet, so they were able to get along quite quickly, even the ground under foot had become firm. They had travelled about three kilometre's, keeping as close to the edge of the bushes as possible. As the crops in this field were quite tall and as long as they were quiet, no-one would know they were there.

Moving at a good pace, listening for any sounds or signs of those in pursuit, the only sound they could hear was that of the cockerel which seemed to be getting louder with every step they made.

Eventually they came to a gap in the hedgerow and a gate leading on to a narrow lane, well kept and clear of any weeds or young saplings. Across this lane, another gate leading to a little plot of land well laid out and organised.

"Surely someone must live around here?" said Joe.

Yet everything seemed so still and quite, except for the cockerel and the noise of the kitchen door slamming with every gust of the morning breeze. All they could see was the back of the house and the outhouses and the door that was left swinging with each gust of the wind.

The place looked deserted, but they were too frightened to step out into the open, just in case someone was there watching.

They had the feeling, there was something wrong here.

For ages they stayed hidden under the bushes, waiting for any signs of movement or life. No-one seemed to be around the farm looking after the animals, and there were a good variety of vegetables growing unattended in a little patch of land to one side of the house.

Standing alone, the house and all the ground around it had been well maintained, it was surrounded by the forest, the only way to reach it would be by the lane and a narrow path leading down to the tow-path.

Well-cultivated patches of land were covered with bushes, all loaded with all different types of fruits, a small orchard of medium-sized trees occupied a fair piece of the land. From their position they could see the house itself was a good size and would accommodate quite a few people. There seemed a great many windows on the ground floor as far as they could see, the upstairs windows were set into the tiled roof, spaced between the many tall chimneys. A huge shrub of the Wisteria with its light blue flowers covered most of the external walls of the house.

None of the group wanted to move, they were quite happy just to feast on the scene in front of them for the time being.

Then they all noticed the mounds of earth on top of these mounds were six little crosses, but there was another pile of earth without a cross. Curiosity drew them out from beneath the bushes, they could not understand the significance of the piles of earth or the crosses. They had never seen anything like it before.

Only Tom knew their significance.

As they approached, keeping a eye open for any sign of movement, a large number of rats came running out of the ground near the seventh pile. As they drew near, they could see that a hole had been dug.

"I've read somewhere that sometimes, instead of burning the bodies, they bury them," said Tom.

"Why?" asked Mike.

"It's what they believe. Something to do with religion and, as I've said, it's what some of the people believed in."

Tom felt a little self-conscious trying to explain himself.

He had been thinking a lot since his old friend had given him the book of the *New Testament and Psalms*.

"This is in preparation for another burial," he added, before anyone could say anything. But they all understood.

Still the rats came running, scattering all over the place heading for the safety of the forest.

When they reached the edge of the hole, looking down they could see the remains of what was the body of a half-eaten man, he was lying in a position as if he had been just waiting to die.

"I only hope he died before the rats got to him," Steve remarked.

"It looks like he's been dead for a week or more, well before the rats and other animals arrived," answered Jim.

While some went off to have a look at the other mounds, Ken and Len volunteered to go and find something that would cover the poor man's remains. After a while they came back carrying an old door that they had they had found.

They began filling the hole in with the soil that had been piled up alongside. Tom and Jim wandered off towards the house after offering to help fill in the grave: Ken said they could manage.

"We will go and have look around the main house," said Jim, not knowing what they may find.

While Steve headed over to a group of outhouses that stood well away from the main house, he wanted to see if he could find anything that may be useful.

As Tom and Jim wandered over towards the house, still keeping a watchful eye on the windows, wondering if there were any other people living here or nearby.

As they approached the building Steve shouted over, warning them to be careful and to keep a look out.

It was only when Mike started poking at one of the mounds, interested in what they were, that Tom shouted over: "There may be bodies under the earth. So be careful. See if there are any names or dates on the crosses."

Leo, in the meantime, had gone to check over what livestock there was and what they were kept in. He found six or seven sheep wandering around an open space, with a few of this year's lambs mixed with a few goats of all ages. In a couple of sties there were pigs.

But as he came to explore the area more closely, he found to his horror, several rotting carcasses.

He had seen animals die before, but had never seen so many die together in so short a time or being left to rot. Thinking that they must have only been dead two or more weeks by the state of the bodies, and with the graves – was there any connection between their deaths and those people in the graves, if so what had caused them all to die?

Turning his attention back to the house, Tom heeded Steve's warning and wedged the door open, making sure that if there was anyone around he would have an escape route.

Happy now with the knowledge that if need be, he could escape easily, he slowly entered the first room which he took to be the kitchen, with a red-tiled floor and a huge sink that occupied the space by the window. A large fridge freezer covered the opposite wall, and loads of cupboards.

But this was Jacob's territory he thought.

As he was about to go and explore the other rooms, Jacob entered with his large knapsack and started going through some of the wall cupboards, looking for any food there was that they could take with them.

Tom noticed that he had already filled one of their bags. When Jacob saw Tom looking, he said:

"These were tins of various fruits, tinned meats and soups."

"That'll keep us going for a few days at least," replied Tom.

Leaving Jacob to carry on, Tom was keen to explore the rest of the house.

He went through a rather small door into a very large open space, that he imagined to be the main room of the house; chairs placed in no particular way filled the room, in one of the corners was a large clock, still ticking away telling no-one the time.

One half of the main wall was completely taken up by shelves filled with books.

He had never seen so many books covering all different topics. He went over to get a better look, it was only when he was close did he realise that the shelves would normally be hidden from view by a wooden panel that had been folded back so as to gain access to the shelves.

*But why would they need to be hidden?* Tom thought to himself.

A large table occupied a large proportion of the space in the middle of the room, it was crammed full with papers and a few books, but one book stood alone. It looked different to any of the others, or any on the shelves. A dirty cup and a plate with a meal half-finished had been pushed to the side, as if the writer realised that they had no-more time, their time had come.

Skipping through the pages, Tom soon realised that whoever it was that had written this book had immaculate handwriting skills.

The cover of the book was handmade out of some kind of soft animal skin, and the person who had done the lettering on the cover had taken their time, it was beautify done.

Now as he began to read through the pages, Tom knew that this was about a family, whoever they were, and this was about their daily lives, and would hopefully explain what had caused their deaths and about those in the graves outside and the way they had died.

Lying flat on the table was a photograph of the family: the man, a woman, four girls and a boy.

Beginning with the first to fall ill, little Rosy the youngest of the daughters. She was only four years old, our little darling even Ron spoilt her, he was our only boy he would be next at the tender age of seven, it wasn't long before Gillian and Julie, the twins, fell ill on the same day, at just eleven years of age. Shortly after it claimed Margaret, the eldest, followed by Ann my wife, two days later, the heartache is too much to bear, I know it will not be long before it will be my turn.

I've dug my own grave and I pray that it will not be long so that I may join my family, my only hope is that someone will come by and throw some of the soil over, and cover me.

At the top of the page the man had written in

large capital letter's IT HAD RETURNED SO GOD HELP US. What did the man mean by that? Tom had no idea.

Reading through the pages it told of how it all began.

Looking at the photo Tom tried to imagine all the family playing together on a warm summer's day, what each of the children was like. It was on the first of August when the two youngest came across an old tramp lying on the canal towpath, not far from the house. It had been raining the night before, yet all he wore was some dirty old rags which were soaking wet, he himself was very dirty.

The children could see that he was very ill, so they ran and fetched their mother, together they brought him back to the farm, even though the old man had protested strongly, telling them that they must not go near him, and to leave him there. But she knew that if he was left he would die. She could not just leave him, she could not have that on her conscience. After a while he began to explain that he had come across some yellow plastic bags that may have been buried or hidden many years previous, and probably had been uncovered by some animal scavenging for food. He had no idea what was in the bags or what they contained. One of the bags had been ripped open, inside there was a few bandages and swabs, and one or two syringes. He had tried to bury them the best as he could, but after a day he began to feel unwell.

Even with our help, he had died two days later. they had taken his body well into the forest and buried it there covering the grave with boulders so it would not be disturbed. At least we had done our best.

Three days later our kindness was to be repaid, our troubles had began and it was young Rose that went down with the illness first, caught from the man they had helped. At first we had no idea what it was but as each day passed Rosy got worse, then after reading through book after book, paper after paper we began to realise what it was that we had brought into our house, god forgive us.

Now we realised why he had warned them to leave him, but now it was too late and it was not long before we all began to feel unwell. I've buried my family, now I have all the signs, so it will not be long.

What to make of it Tom had no idea, what had returned and what had he meant by god help us. He was still thinking about it when Steve came in looking pleased with himself.

"I've found something useful if we ever encounter those guards again."

"Here," he said, motioning to the others, "look what I've got."

"What is it?" asked Mike, giving the object in Steve's hand a curious look.

Holding firmly onto the crossbow and bolts, Steve told them: "It's a crossbow."

Tom looked on from a distance. He didn't want to touch them.

They looked lethal.

They could hear Ken and Len outside. They were finishing off burying the man's remains.

Jacob entered from the kitchen carrying his large bag of tinned food.

Tom smiled to himself as Jacob emptied the contents on the table.

"You must be thinking that we are going to last out here for quite a while yet?" he said, laughing at the amount of tins.

Steve came over to the table checking the tins.

Jim, Mike and Joe, who had been going over the upper floor rooms, came down with a armful of the dead man's clothes. Luckily he had been roughly the same height and build so now they could change some of their wet clothes, all except Steve who was much bigger and towered over all of them.

Ken and Len came in carrying two bags of fresh vegetables and fruit. Steve looked at the bags, then at all the tins on the table, then with a smile asked Jacob:

"How long do you think we'll be out here?"

They all smiled. They knew they'd been lucky getting even this far. Tom could not get that book out of his thoughts even when everyone seemed jovial. Soon they would have to be on the move, so he decided to fetch that book.

"Where's Joe?" Jim asked.

"I think he's looking after the animals. He wasn't too happy when I looked out of the window," said Jacob.

"I think something's wrong with a few of them."

As they made their way to go and see what the trouble was, Joe came in and they could tell by the look on his face that something was troubling him.

"What's the matter? Are you alright?" Ken asked.

"Some of the animals have died. They were just

lying there. So I've buried them. And a couple of the goats needed milking."

Holding three containers full of the warm creamy liquid, there was just a hint of a smile.

Gathering all the loot together, they knew it was time to be on the move. There was something here that made them feel uneasy, plus those chasing them were probably already on the move by now. And how far behind they were, nobody knew. So, the sooner they left, the better. What chance did they have if they came face-to-face with their pursuers? Even with Steve's crossbow he had found, and he would soon run out of ammunition for his gun, they would be no match against the guns of the guards.

Seeing what had happened to Mark and Phil, some were of the opinion that they'd need something else to arm themselves with. After a couple of minutes, Leo said:

"I've seen the things we need, round the back of the house."

Leaving the others to search for anything that could be of use, he went out, returning within a short time with four or five rods of steel – about one hundred and thirty centimetres long; twelve millimetres wide: all with razor-sharp point at one end.

"They were part of a fence," he added. "They rusted and fell apart. They may do as weapons."

Packing everything they could carry into bags, they wanted to be out of here as soon as they could.

The place was beginning to play on their nerves.

Tom put the book away into his bag.

Before leaving, they stopped to have one last look at the seven mounds of earth. Each had a wooden cross and, engraved in the wood, the name and age of the deceased.

Taking out the little red book he had been given many years ago, and most mornings he would have read a little from it, he now began to read a few words. THE LORDS MY SHEPHERD I WILL NOT WANT. While he read on the others remained silent, remembering the same feeling of sadness when they lost their two companions, Mark and Phil.

When he had finished he bent down by the cross that one of them had made, and with his knife scratched the name Peter in the soft wood. He got the name off the back of the photo.

Now it was time to move on. They were all keen to be away from this place, hidden from the outside world by the forest of trees surrounding it, but it was the one place they hoped their pursuers would find for the sake of the remaining animals.

Fully loaded with everything that they thought would be handy, but not too much as to slow them down.

Not wanting to hang about any longer they were on their way.

After walking for about two hours, they came to a section of the canal where it split once again, going off in different directions: one seemingly headed south, the other kept going in an easterly direction. Across from the junction, where the canals split, they could just make out what looked like workshops. Normally, they imagined that this area would be very busy with narrowboats being loaded and unloaded. But today was a Sunday so no-one was around.

While Jim and the others kept an eye open for any narrowboats coming their way, Tom and Steve were about to investigate what the real purpose of these buildings was, when a door on the side of one of the buildings opened.

A man came out, then a strange vehicle came down a slight incline and pulled up opposite the man. It only had three wheels: one underneath a small cabin at the front; the other two were fitted to the back trailer, on which there were several parcels. The driver and the man seemed to be waiting for someone.

Minutes later, they heard the familiar sound of a narrowboat coming along the canal – from the direction that they had just travelled. As the sound increased, they could see the boat coming around the corner. A young girl at the tiller, guided the boat skillfully towards the jetty where the driver and the man had been waiting.

A young man jumped from the lead boat onto the two boats that it was towing. As they came alongside the jetty, he threw a rope round a Ballard on the side of the jetty. Bringing all the boats to a halt alongside the jetty, enabling them to unload and load.

Impressed by how smoothly the whole thing had gone, the group decided to take the path going east, not wishing to stay too long in the same area. They knew that if they stayed here too long, they'd be caught.

Soon it would be time to start thinking about where they were going to sleep.

The house had been out of question, there was something about it that still worried them.

They had spent more time at that house than they intended to, and as the fourth day drew to a close, they had a lot to think about. It wouldn't be too bad if they had to sleep out in the open as it was quite warm and the sky looked promising, so they carried on till it started to get to dark to see where they were going.

Here there seemed to be several docks all in a line. At different levels several narrow boats were tied up alongside, two or three had lights on with tufts of smoke drifting from their small chimneys.

Walking quickly, they were keen to get past them, worried just in case someone came out.

It wasn't until they came across a piece of open ground, hidden from view by a tall hedge, that they decided that it would be alright to stay there for the night.

Once they were happy that they hadn't been seen, Jacob began to sort out what food they had taken from the farm.

While the rest split into two groups, some went to find dry wood, the rest went to explore the best direction to take at daybreak – the two groups going in different directions along the towpath.

Under the stars this is what they had given their lives for, to be free from orders, to be able to make their own decisions right or wrong. It would be their choice.

After a good meal and everything was put away, they all lay on the warm ground looking up at all the stars and were soon fast asleep.

Earlier that morning, Margaret Storrs (and the others) had awoken early. She wanted to be on the move and meet up with the captain's men who had stayed out and made camp with the sergeant.

The captain had brought them back to the governor's for the night.

She wanted to see if there had been any news of the whereabouts of those men because she had heard that London was getting impatient and would be sending someone up to sort out the problem.

To her disappointment, they were all summoned back to the council offices immediately.

Leaving Captain Turner to go and join his men, and try his idea of putting a sentry on every bridge crossing the canals and roads in the area where the fugitives were thought to be heading.

He had realised that they had been going in a south easterly direction, criss-crossing the canals and roads, so he would set the trap while he and the remaining guards would give chase.

# 10

After having getting a few hours sleep under the cover of the small copse of young trees, and a hearty breakfast, the nine men moved off across the open fields, hoping that it was far too early for anyone to be up and about. Even the sun hadn't risen.

They could just make lights on in the windows of a farmhouse – far away in the distance.

Flocks of birds, nesting in the trees, were just waking, singing loud enough to awaken the dead. In the distance, they could hear a cockerel giving his wake-up call. It was dawn.

They watched a light from the farmhouse as the door opened and closed, away on the other side of the field. After a second or two another much bigger door opened into an outer building and with the door open they could hear a strange bellowing echoing from within.

Leo laughed at the looks on his companions' faces.

"It was just the cattle being milked," he said. "You've heard them before."

He continued:

"I wish I could've worked on a farm looking after cows and sheep out in the open air all day, like those we saw yesterday."

"Yes but we were stuck inside every hour of the day," said Jim, impatient to be on the move again and get back under the cover of the hedgerows before it got too light. This was their fifth day.

All day long they kept on the move under the cover of the hedges, keeping a lookout for anyone coming their way.

By late afternoon they were all tired out from walking in the hot sun. Deciding it was time to have a rest. Sitting in a field of tall barley, they watched as a young couple came into the field and lay down not far from where they were resting. Not daring to move or make a sound in case the young couple heard and realised their presence, raising the alarm and notifying the authorities. For over an hour all they could do was watch fascinated as the pair began to strip off summer clothes, both boy and the girl began to groan with anticipation as the boy's hands began to wander over the girl's body, softly stroking her lower belly.

Suddenly the boy was on top with the girl wrapping her legs around the lower part of his torso, holding him firmly to her, pulling him even closer, the movement of their bodies moved quicker and quicker until suddenly coming to a frenzied climax, exhausted they just lay there held in a sleepy embrace both to tied to cover themselves.

It would be another twenty minutes before the pair

decided to make move. Any longer Tom would have sworn Jim would have done something, but eventually they went off along the towpath, happily holding hands, not realising that their every move had been watched.

"What was that all about?" asked Steve. Again it was left for Leo to explain most of his life had been spent, alone amongst his animals and had often witnessed the animals mating making just as much noise, but not with so much enthusiasm.

Jim shouted that over, in the far corner he could see some movement, a farmer was bringing what to them looked a fierce cow into the nearby field. "I think that we had better get out of here fast," said Leo. "I believe that's a bull."

Following Leo's example, all of them made a quick dash for the gate, and by this time they were quite exhausted and were ready to settle down. By then it was early evening, so taking a slow walk alongside a dried up lane, in the warmth of the sun help them to relax a little, the performance in the field had affected them all, without any of them really knowing why.

As the evening went by they decided to call it a day and find somewhere to camp for the night. It was still quite warm with a refreshing breeze drafting across the fields and along the towpath of the canal. After jumping over the gate earlier, they had enough for one day.

They had just found somewhere to hide amongst tall bushes that would help protect them if the weather did turn for the worse, when they heard music coming from a house on the other side of the canal, set well back from the water's edge. On a large grassed area separating the house from the canal was a large marquee lit up by all the lights inside, hiding most of the house from their view, so the little group could watch what was going on without fear of being seen.

Curious at what was going on, they made their way over to the otherside by way of a set of lock gates, leading down to where the canal was much lower.

The side of the canal had been cut away, making a small dock, which housed a small pleasure boat.

They were well hidden, in the shadows of the bushes, but not wanting to take the risk of any of the guests venturing down and discovering they hid well into the shadows. Amongst the tall bushes they could see if any one did wander down without the fear of being seen, with the falling sun it would soon be dark. They were just about to leave, when they saw two young men.

Estimating their ages to be between eighteen and twenty and they were heading in their direction.

As they made their way down across the grassy area well away from the house and the remainder party, the taller of the pair seemed to be pulling a young girl along with him.

The second lad was shouting at the first, protesting wildly as if disagreeing. Well hidden in the thick bushes, as they watched, they could see that the girl was distressed, yet she neither shouted nor called out for assistance, from those at the house.

Even though the lad was shouting at the other, who by now had the girl pinned down on the grass, pulling at her clothes, he did nothing, only walk off up towards the house, not bothering to raise the alarm, or to help the girl, she was left at the mercy of his friend.

The group watched horrified at the scene, this was different to what they had witnessed earlier. There was no excitement on the girl's face only terror and panic; her mouth was working yet no sound left her lips, as he ripped away at her under garments.

So intent was her attacker on what he was doing, that he had not heard the sound of the hedge being parted or the crack of the twigs under foot as the man stepped out of hiding and moved quickly towards him.

Only the girl saw the figure standing behind her assailant, her eyes wide open in shear panic, not knowing what to expect or what was about to happen, still no sound left her lips.

Nor could she warn the lad.

Neither had the lad realised at what was about to happen next, he was so engrossed in his vicious attack and rape of the girl, not until he felt the hand as it went around his mouth pulling his head back and muffling out any sound or cry.

Now he felt and knew the panic the girl was enduring, as he felt the sharp point of the iron railing being pushed through cotton shirt, skin and flesh piercing the aorta.

It was the girl's turn to see the terror on the lad's face, the hand stopped any scream from leaving his mouth, she saw the red stain spreading over the clean white shirt forming a pattern and the spike that seemed to grow even larger out of the boy's chest.

The others had kept well hidden, still not realising what had just happened. It was Tom's first kill; all the hatred was behind it, partly in revenge for the killing of their two friends, also the brutal attack on the girl, and the thought of all those years of being locked away for nothing.

Tom pulled the body off the girl and let it fall to the ground, as if it was a bag of potatoes, and helped the girl to her feet standing back, while she had pulled her clothes straight. He tried to explain that it would be best for her to go with them as it would not be safe for her to stay and to explain what had happened to the boy.

At first they thought that she was too frightened and shocked to speak, then realised that she could not.

She was frightened to move, but after a few minutes and with Tom's help slowly she began to relax and follow him. She too had come to realise that it would be impossible for her to stay.

Jim called over and said:

"Get a move on before the other one comes back to see what's had happened to his friend."

They were just in time to hear the lad calling out from the house.

Mike and Steve in the meantime had carried the body of the dead man down to the side of the canal, after filling all his pockets and the legs of his trousers with heavy stones, without the slightest noise dropped the body into the mucky waters of the lock.

While Tom had been trying to find out what she was doing there without much success. It was Mike who realised the problem and came to the rescue. With just a few hand signs, soon found out that she had been a servant at the house with two other girls, none of them could talk. They are what was classed as dumb, but after a time they had been taught this sign language.

He also found out that her name was Rose and that they lived in a room above the stables at the back of the main house where the party was being held. They were celebrating the owner's daughter finishing university.

"Who were the two lads that attacked you?" asked Tom.

"They were just friends of the daughter," answered the girl.

They found out, all they could about the people that lived there and what it was like.

With every bit of information having to be passed between Mike, Tom and Rose it was hard work.

Tom remembered that it had been Joe that he had seen reading the flashes of light from the other buildings, and recalled seeing Mike, Len and Ken doing those very hand signs to each other in the noisy machine shops where they worked. Tom asked Mike: "Could he teach him some of the hand signs, so he could talk to Rose direct?"

Moving as fast as they could across the field, that had been baked hard by the afternoon sun trying to get away from there, before anyone from the party came to help the boy look for his friend, or any eyes that happened to be around. Deciding that it would be better to leave the paths alone for a while and as the moon gave a silvery glow they thought it better to stay under the cover of the hedges and trees, yet parts of the field that had been sheltered from the sun were still wet from the storm two nights ago.

"It may help throw our pursuers off for a while," said Steve.

By the time they crossed the field they were exhausted. After a brief stop decided that they were still to close, If they had started looking for the boy then the whole area would be flooded with people, so they kept on moving for another hour by which time it was getting pitch black under the hedges, even though out in the open fields by the light of the moon it was bright.

They began to find it impossible to see where they were going under the shadows of the trees. Deciding that they should be safe now to walk along the towpath again. With them all looking for a place to rest up for the night, they were not watching the towpaths further along or the bridges above.

But unknown to them they had been seen, by a lone figure standing in the shadows on the bridge above them. He had been watching them all the way along, now he took careful aim as Joe walked into his sights.

When the first bullet hit Joe he did not know what had happened. The top right half of his torso was taken away as the sniper's snub-nosed bullet found its mark.

Joe's body was spun around with the impact before falling over the edge into the murky water of the canal below. This had been the little group's first mistake, forgetting that there would be people out there waiting for them to appear.

Now it would be the sniper's turn to make that one and only fatal mistake In the excitement of his first kill, all his thoughts were on his next targets. He removed all his protective headgear to be able to see his targets more clearly.

He had not seen the figure hidden away in the shadows, but the figure had heard and seen the flash as he had fired. The sniper's luck had ran out; if only that figure had not been Steve whose actions were swift as he stepped out of the shadows – it was too late. The bolt from the crossbow ripped through the sniper's throat.

Before the body had hit the ground he was dead, the life blood being pumped out of his body.

Steve and Jim moved quickly up the bank wanting to make sure the man was dead, and to see if he was alone. Once they were on the bridge, they could see it was obvious he was dead, and that he had been alone.

Bending down Steve retrieved the bolt, also the soldier's automatic pistol with all the ammunition.

Steve also noticed that in his haste the man had not made any attempt to get in touch with base, his phone was still in it's pocket, which meant no- one would know where they were or what had happened.

Meanwhile, the rest of the group were waiting at the side of the canal, waiting to see if it was safe to come out of hiding, and if there were was anything that could be done for poor Joe. But as the body drifted to the surface motionless, and the water in the lock had began to turn red, they knew there was nothing they could do.

This was their third member to be killed, now there were only eight. Up on the bridge Steve explained:

"No-one will know we're here until they come to see why he has not been in touch. The sooner we're on our way the better."

"So if the man has not been in touch with anyone then there's a good chance that they don't know where we are either?" Jim asked. "And if that is the case we are as safe here as anywhere?"

They all agreed he had a point but, Steve disagreed, saying: "If anyone else is out there they would have heard the shots and will certainly come looking. They will at least enquire and do a roll call and when he doesn't answer this area will soon be swarming with troops."

Now it had become a game of cat and mouse, even though the end was certain and could be predicted.

But something new could be felt within the group, they had began to enjoy this new-found freedom and the feeling of excitement. It would be good just to feel alive for once, and be one step ahead for as long as they could. With their new-found knowledge, combined with the feeling that they were not completely helpless Steve said: "I think it would be a good idea, for all of you to learn how to use both guns and the crossbow."

While he was busy showing Jim and Leo how to aim and fire each of the weapons, Ken, Mike and Len, under the cover of the shadows, returned down to the side of the canal, and retrieved Joe's body before they were on the move again.

By the light of the moon the three men stood in silence, looking down at the body of their friend floating in the mucky water of the lock, working out how would be the best way to get down. It was then Mike noticed the metal ladder sunk into the brickwork of the lock. Their problem now was how they were going to get Joe's body out of the lock.

The level was right down and if they opened either gate Joe's body may be washed into the middle, so they would try and lift the body out. While Mike climbed down, Len and Ken went in search of something to lift the body out of the water.

After a few minutes they came across a box fixed to a post on the side of the path. Inside was a canvas belt with a good length of rope, the very thing they wanted.

Mike had managed to grab the body before it sank to the bottom, but he was struggling to keep hold of it with just one hand, while holding onto the rung of the ladder with the other. He was relieved when the lifebelt on the end of the rope dangled beside him. In no time at all Joe's body was lying on the towpath.

Another five minutes and the three of them had joined the rest, leaving the body where it would certainly be found, hopefully by one of the boatmen or someone travelling along the canal towpath before daybreak.

Even though they were all completely exhausted, they knew that Steve had been right and they must be on their way and keep going and get out of this area as quick as possible.

Dawn would be upon them in a couple of hours so they must move as fast as their legs could take them.

Poor Rose they thought, but to their surprise she kept up with them, nor did she complain.

Hoping that by the time anyone was up and about, they would have found somewhere to rest for a few hours out of sight.

**11**

Back at the council offices in Birmingham, Margaret Storrs and Dr Caroline weren't too happy at been ordered back while the fugitives were still at large. They had been shown to chairs around the large table, which John and Yvonne both remembered from the last time they had been summoned here. Until now John had not thought any more about that map behind the door, but looking over his shoulder he could see it had been exchanged with a huge painting, it was of men sitting in a group. At first he thought it could be the famous painting of *The Night Watch*, by Rembrandt ,but it could not be, not hanging here.

Before he had the chance to take a closer look, they were all told to take their seats at the table.

Margaret Storrs took the chair at the head of the table. When they were all seated Mark Sykes stood up, demanding to know the reason why they had all been summoned back here, and what action was being taken now to capture those men while we are sitting here?

"Please tell me what had been done, while you were

there?" It was one of the men John remembered that was at the very first meeting, but not in the second meeting or the search.

Not allowing anyone to answer he continued.

"I see that all the mediums have been instructed to inform the public that a gang of criminals have escaped from a detention zone. And that there has been reports coming in that a family of seven has been murdered by this group of escaped prisoners. And they should inform the authorities if there is any sighting of them. There must be no contact with them on no account."

"The family had been discovered not long after the fugitives had fled," said Sykes, who had not been slow to see his opportunity and had taken Captain Turner's advice and ordered that the whole area be surrounded with Margaret's own armed men. Now all they had to do was wait until someone spots them, then the forces standing by could go in and capture them. It would be that easy.

Yvonne wasn't that sure it would be that easy, interrupting Sykes by saying: "I do not understand how on earth have these men, none of which has had any idea of the terrain, for the last couple of days they have been walking about as if on a Sunday stroll."

Stopping just to see what the reaction was.

There was none. They just waited knowing there was more to come.

"If that was not enough they're always keeping one step ahead of us at all time and they've been out there for three days. We thought they must be hungry, cold and wet, and these men were none of those." She sat down in her chair angry with herself because she then realised that she had put both of them in a very dangerous position.

Sykes quickly interrupted her by correcting the term men, in his eyes they were still just talking machines.

Yvonne was livid, looking straight into his eyes, at no-one else, fighting to keep back the anger she could feel inside, she asked him.

"If those are talking machines as you would like to call them, how come they do and go where they like? If they were only capable of doing things they were only programmed to do, and were not able to think rashly, then how is it for three days they have moved about the area so easily?"

Now she was in full flow she was wild with anger. "And another thing," she shouted at Sykes, "if they had killed that family why would they bother to bury them and why would machines put a cross on their graves?" He had no answers, and the look on the faces of the others sitting around the table, told her she had been right. Maybe now they would give more credit to those men.

Now it was Margaret Storrs' turn to speak.

"No matter what you say those men are dangerous and are *Beyond Salvage* and will be liquidated as soon as they are caught. The zone where they escaped from will have to be inspected thoroughly."

She had not taken her eyes off John and Yvonne all the time she had been speaking.

"If anything is found they will all have to be liquidated," she added.

"But what would you be looking for? Nothing goes in or out, only that which is ordered and that is inspected before it's sent and when it arrives, and whatever news they hear is whatever you want them to hear, another thing me and Sykes here went and had a good look around and found nothing." Now it was John's turn to face her.

She faced no-one, just stared at the paintings hanging around the walls, Whatever she was thinking no-one could tell.

Everyone turned to face John, keen to hear if he had anything more to say. But he waited, not wanting to say too much until he had time to think about it. Then and only then would he open his mouth.

But there was still one thing that bothered him since they had visited the production zone the first time.

"There is one question I would like to ask all of you here," he said.

"As Mark as pointed out before, if these men had never seen a woman before, how come when we entered the machine shops at that production zone, they seemed to be attracted only to the women?" Pointing out the three women sitting around the table: "And they seemed to be very interested in Dr Caroline."

Dr Caroline was beautiful with her long red hair and green eyes, and the fragrance of her perfume filled the room. She knew that whenever she entered a room men noticed, even John could not help looking.

"How could they have possibly know that there was a difference between the sexes?"

Suddenly another member of the group spoke up. His hair was as dark as night just beginning to show signs of grey at the temples, he was well built and when he did speak he spoke with what they thought to be a slight Italian accent. Neither John nor Yvonne had ever seen him before today.

He spoke for the first time since they had sat at the table.

He never attempted to introduce himself, looking directly at John he said:

"If what you are implying is only fractionally true then we have a problem. It maybe some of these men are getting information by some other means and that will be our first priority. Once these men have been caught, alive if possible, we must find out if they had received help. Underestimating these men could be our biggest mistake, not realising or treating them as men, and women as well may I point out that can still think logically, and they are not just machines. We taught them how to work out problems for us so we have only ourselves to blame."

Continuing to keep his eyes fixed on John, but John noticed there was just a hint of mischief hiding in those dark brown eyes, ready to pick up any flaw in their statements.

"As you asked John, was it that they looked so different, or could it also be that they are getting information from some other source, and that would be a worry, because all unauthorised books have been banned, so we would have to look into how they have learnt so much?

"By the way my name is Karl Ferris I've been sent down from Brussels to investigate what is happening here. At the moment we're trying to keep these things out of the press, about these men having escaped from a Work Zone. When we do let the public know it would be a couple of convicts who have escaped from a prison that have killed the family."

He looked over towards Sykes, who nodded in acknowledgement.

By now Storrs had lost it, getting up from her chair she stormed around the room only stopping when she reached where Sykes sat, then leaning over his shoulder.

She spoke loud enough for everyone to hear, so as to warn all of them in the room.

"It may not be just our cushy jobs that we lose, if these men are not caught soon, and I would make sure that you two are included."

John felt the hairs on the back of his neck stand up, at the looks she gave him and Yvonne. He wondered what they had done to upset her so much, god only knew.

Then it was the new guy Karl's turn to be in her focus, but to the surprise of the others when she spoke to him, her voice was soft, and she even smiled.

John thought that maybe, just maybe, there was more to the stranger than they first realised, He could have more power than any of them had thought. And what was going on between the two of them? No-one had heard what she had said, yet he seemed to agree on what she had said though by his body language.

John looked around the rest of the table to see what their reactions were, but no-one was going to give anything away especially in front of Storrs. If only he could get one of them aside after the meeting, he may find out something about this new guy Karl and who he was or where he came from.

There was something about him that said he was not English nor was he European. John even thought that he could be Egyptian or from somewhere around that region.

It was then that Sykes called the meeting to order and started by pressing the point that it was due to him that the whole area had been closed down to prevent those prisoners, who were still alive, from being able to breaking out of the security ring.

With the media's warning, everyone in the circle will now be looking out for them to receive the reward of 2000 units that had been offered.

"So I do not think that it will be too long before we hear something," bragged Sykes, pleased with himself that he got one over the others.

"I hope so," was Karl Ferris's reply.

"What do we think was the real cause for the whole family to die so close together, and please do not tell us they were murdered, we can see by the evidence in those reports that there is no signs of any foul play other than on the father, and that was due to rats and other wild animals eating away at the torso before it was buried?"

This was a different member of the group, who nobody had bothered to acknowledge beforehand. She looked a young girl, everyone had thought that she was a secretary, part of the administration. By the slight smile on her pretty face she knew what everyone had been thinking.

"May I introduce myself: I'm Detective Inspector Jillian Dove."

They were all taken by surprise, no-one had expected this. Who had called the police or told anyone outside this area? But now they just sat in silence waiting for the inspector to explain.

But she wanted answers not questions, and she would not be intimidated by them. She did not have to explain.

"We don't really know inspector what happened. The bodies are at the morgue right this very minute; we're waiting to hear from the coroner's office, but up till now they are as much in the dark as we are.

"But they have said the answers to your questions should not take long."

It was Dr Caroline who faced the young inspector.

Dr Caroline continued but there was a distinct change to her tone, as if a doubt and been planted.

"All we can do at the moment is to wait and hope we catch these men soon because if this family died from something which could be contagious, and they buried the body and are still wandering about the countryside, this would be something that is not worth thinking about.

"Do you understand what I'm saying inspector?"

Now the smile had gone from the pretty face, and she thought it was time to explain.

"If you would like to know how we learnt the tragic news of dead family, it was a narrowboat skipper who had seen a group of men coming out of the woods where he knew the family lived. He stopped to investigate what they had been up to, but when he found the graves, he then reported to us that a gang of men had murdered a family of seven.

"We had no idea who these men, and I underline the word men, were, but no matter what you would like to call them under the law they are still men, and will be protected by the law." The inspector would not be bullied by anyone.

"But that does not answer our problem. What would happen if the public got wind of what these men really are?"

They all looked at Karl Ferris who was just making his point and warning them that governments all across the world would have a lot of explaining to do, and they would not like that one bit, because no-one but the authorities knew exactly what went on behind those fences. Not to be warned off the young inspector stood her ground.

"I would also like to know what happened to the other two fugitives because we have been told that eleven had escaped and now you say there are only nine wandering around."

Everyone knew that this inspector was not going to give up that easy.

Everyone looked across to Storrs who said in a whisper: "They are both dead."

"May I ask: how did they died?" said the inspector, not taking her eyes off Storrs for a second, wanting to see what would be the reaction.

But it was Dr Caroline who replied saying that:

"They were eliminated humanely because one was badly injured, and they had become too dangerous, nor would they have been any good for anything." John sensed the good doctor was digging a hole for herself with the inspector.

"What crime had they committed? Did they have a fair trial or do you not think that they have the same rights has all the rest of us?" asked the inspector.

"No they are not entitled," answered Sykes. The Director of Production had had enough of this young whippersnapper, and wanted to put her in her place. His voice was raised an octave as he glared at the inspector. "They have no rights. They are just machines."

But that was not the answer the young policewoman wanted to hear, neither was she impressed.

The director soon realised this by the look on her face, and tried to talk his way out of the hole that he had dug for himself without success.

"Some of your colleague's seem to disagree with you there Mr Sykes about them being just machines, and I would find it interesting to see what the court of human rights would have to say about that." she said.

John and Yvonne watched with interest at the determination of the young woman. She was not going to be pushed around by anyone here. And she was also determined to get at the truth about the deaths of the two young men.

It was then the huge doors at the far end were flung open. A man wearing a black suit with a tailed coat announced that dinner was ready, giving Sykes a reprieve.

When they were all seated and waiting for the meal to served, the question of the two men seemed to be forgotten, and the meal seemed to have taken priority.

"Tomorrow's soul objective will be on the capture of those men wandering around the countryside," Margaret Storrs announced.

John soon realised that none of these men were going to survive after they were caught, and felt slightly ashamed at being involved because no-one seemed to know, or were interested in the slightest, what crimes they have ever committed, if any.

It was Jillian Dove who again spoke to ask:

"Are there any images of all those men, so that we will know what they look like, otherwise we may be arresting some innocent person who maybe just wandering around the area at the time?"

"I will see what can be done." It was another member of the party that spoke between mouthfuls of his meal. He wore the uniform of the security guards, but it was different: his was a dark green not the light brown as those of the young captain's squad or that of Margaret Storrs' men. He had not even bothered to introduce himself and nobody dare ask, they just waited to see who he was and what he was going to do. He just sat there by the side of Karl Ferris. Margaret said: "I don't like it one bit, there seems to be too many people getting involved."

Yvonne wondered if it was a part of their training to be so rude, biting her lips to stop her saying something that she would regret later.

No-one said a word, just waited to see if the stranger was going to add anymore to his statement, but the man, who was very tall and looked as if he spent all of his free time in the gym, stayed silent.

The stranger sitting by Karl Ferris just looked at all those assembled around the table, one by one, then he spoke in such a low voice they were hard pressed to hear what he said.

"I felt ashamed that one of my men was among those deserters and I feel bitterly betrayed by this."

"What do you expect me and John to do?" Yvonne asked. "What can we do, or be of any use at all, how can we advise you?"

"For a start you can advise us on how these men think, and what they may do next, because if I am right, are you not both psychologists? Now it is time for you to earn those privileges you get." it was Karl Ferris who answered Yvonne. The look in Karl Ferris's eyes was not just mischievous, it was dangerous.

They were sending out warnings.

"So when we leave here I suggest that all of you go home and think about it because those down in Whitehall are not very impressed with what's going on up here at the moment."

Not letting them have any time to ask any questions he continued.

"It is not just the future of those men, it's all our futures that we should be thinking about. The future of civilisation, because without those men and women in those zones we may not have been able to survive for very long.

"Also because someone down there in London sitting behind a desk has suggested that those men may have somehow been able to acquire some banned literature. If they have we must find out how, and the sooner the better. I've informed those back at the zone that a full inspection of all the buildings must be carried out tonight without fail."

"What will happen to the men if something is found, Margaret?" asked Yvonne.

In a voice full of self-confidence, Margaret told everyone:

"All the residents of the whole block will be liquidated. Does that answer your question, Dr. Dampier?"

"I hope there'll be a trial and an inquest before you do," came his reply.

Now it was the young policewoman's turn again. She seemed concerned at the suggestion that these men were nothing but machines that could be eliminated without any trial on the whim of someone sitting behind a desk. But she was determined that it wouldn't happen on her watch.

After the meal and when they were about to leave, John and Yvonne were taken aside by Dr Caroline who warned them in a whisper.

"All you see and hear in the next few days can't go beyond our little group… because if it did, the consequences would be considerable for us all. I hope I've made myself clear."

Then she focused her gaze on the young inspector who was busy talking to another member of the party who had not bothered to offer any advice on the subject. But John had a feeling that none of this little party could be trusted, nor should they be underestimated.

John could see Margaret Storrs approaching, she also had the inspector in her sights, ignoring both John and Yvonne as she walked past to join Dr Caroline. Keeping their eyes locked on the policewoman, the two women spoke too low for anyone to hear what was being said. It was not to hard to guess what the subject was, and who the intended victim would be. But looks can be deceiving, and now Detective Inspector Jillian Dove understood what had happened to the family, she had also learnt about the two prisoners that had been killed.

Walking over to the far corner of the room where she could be alone, she punched in a number on her phone and within seconds she was speaking to someone.

Whoever it was she was talking to seemed to be in total agreement with what she was saying.

All eyes were fixed on the young inspector now, curious to who she was talking to, and what was being said.

After she had finished the conversation, switching the phone off she rejoined the rest of the party.

"Is everything alright?" asked Karl Ferris.

"Yes, everything's fine," she said. "That was the police commissioner wanting to know what this is all about. He's asked me to stay here with you, until I think fit."

"Pray tell me, what do you intend to do if those men are shot?" asked the stranger in the green uniform. John had noticed that he wore no badges, emblems or insignias to show which forces he belonged or to what authority he answered to.

"That depends on the circumstances. If he's killed because whoever shot him thought their life was in danger, that might be self-defence, but there would still be an inquiry."

"So if captain Turner and his men came across one of these men and he was armed, and believed that their own lives could be in danger, then he would be within their rights to kill, is that what you're saying?"

"Yes," was the short answer from the inspector.

"Some of us here seem to be in two minds as to what goes on in those zones. First, there's the question: is what we do legally right? Secondly, is what we do morally right? But, before we start making any judgements, let us consider the prospects if there were no such places."

Sykes spoke softly. There was no need to shout. There were no points to be gained. He wanted them all to realise the gravity of the situation.

"Sometimes all that's legal isn't just and, sometimes, all that's just isn't legal," was the young inspector's answer.

"Where did you read that, inspector?" asked Karl Ferris.

The mischievous look was back. Was he tormenting the inspector?

"In an old law book written many years ago by a judge, sir."

The "sir" was sharp but polite. The corners of her mouth turned up into a slight smile.

With a bow of his head, Karl Ferris acknowledged defeat in this war of words.

# 12

Most of the men went silently about their business at the zone. They hadn't heard any more about the visitors. They were more concerned with how their friends were managing – wandering about the countryside (not knowing what they were doing or where they were going).

They heard about the commotion it had caused though, and knew it wouldn't be long before the attention turned to them. So the word went round: gather your bags and all banned materials; label them, not with a name, but a mark – so that only the owner could identify who the bag belongs to. Then the bags would be collected and hidden until the fuss died down.

The orders came through. All the buildings were to be searched, not just the one where the men had absconded from. The others were now under the same spotlight.

No-one complained. All they wanted to hear was news of their friends: even if it was bad.

No sooner had the bags of illegal literature been

hidden (only two or three in each building knew where) when the entire building was swarming with men – covered from head to foot in protective gear.

Even their faces couldn't be seen.

They went through every nook and cranny looking for anything that looked suspicious. Their every move was watched attentively by the workers. The time for caring about the consequences had long passed.

After a few hours went by, they still hadn't found anything. Those who had organised the collection had done a good job. Now it was time for the searchers to leave.

Karl Ferris had been in charge of the search and, to the dismay of his men, ordered it to be repeated: twice. In the end, though, even he had to admit there was nothing to find.

(If only they'd checked the huge water tanks on the roofs. There, they'd have found bags tightly sealed in water-tight boxes.)

Those who were responsible for hiding the bags had allowed the water level in the tanks to run low enough to enable them to lower the boxes to the bottom, and then covering the lot with a black plastic sheet, then refilling the tanks again. Looking into the tanks from the top, the boxes couldn't be seen.

Even then, Karl Ferris wasn't too happy leaving. He still believed that there was something amiss here.

Every which way they looked, there was someone watching.

From a distance, there was always one of the men

standing alone, watching. They would soon know if they had found anything, but now realised that they'd missed something and that these men were just laughing at them. From the roof they watched as Karl Ferris and his men went aboard the narrowboat that was to take them back into town.

Sitting alone at the front of the narrowboat, Karl Ferris was furious. He realised that everything back at the zone had been cleverly planned. In the fugitives' case he believed, they were just going wherever they fancied, zing zagging over fields and canals.

"We've no chance of knowing where they'll turn up, do we, Captain" he said, as the latter sat down beside him.

"No," was the captain's reply.

It didn't bother Karl Ferris in the least he had been happy to have joined the captain and his men out there in the open. But now back in the office he thought it would be very interesting if they could only capture one, just to talk to one of those men. It might give them a clue just how much they knew before Storrs got hold of them. She was far too trigger happy for his liking, she was too hasty to punish without stopping to think.

What did trouble him though, was what if the very same thing was happening in other building at other sites all over the country, even the world.

If that was the case then we could be in trouble if we didn't change.

Back at the offices John came over and stood next to Karl, who had been standing alone thinking of the consequences if such a thing was possible. He shook his head not wanting to even think about it.

But it would not go away.

He had been back at the office for two hours now, and it was getting late, so it had been decided not to bother chasing after the fugitives tonight, nothing would be gained.

Both men stood by each other's side in silence pondering over what would be the fugitives next move, when they were joined by Sykes. For a few minutes the three of men did not speak.

Then Karl asked Sykes.

"How many days had they been on the loose, and why were we not informed about that first visit to the site?" without stopping for breath he turned to face John.

"By the way, did you know about that, John?"

John had to think hard and fast before deciding that telling the truth was the best way to go.

"Yes, we were all there, weren't we, Mark?"

"This will be their fourth day on the run, and we've just heard that another body's been found", Sykes said, addressing neither man in particular.

"And, there's also a report of a boy and a servant girl missing."

"Near where the body was found?" asked Karl.

"They were at a party being held at a property on the edge of the same canal and in the same area where the fugitives were last seen."

"Do you think they're dead. Is there any connection?"

There was a look of concern on Karl's face. He turned to John and asked him:

"Was there any chance that these men were out on some kind of revenge killing spree?"

Now it was John's turn to be concerned. After a few moments thought, he decided that telling the truth would be the best option.

He decided to hell with it saying *'he didn't think so'* and *'that he thought It was just circumstances that was driving them on'*.

With a nod of his head Karl seemed to agree that it was circumstances more that anything that drove the fugitives on.

John said: "I honestly thought that when they first escaped they never had an ounce of revenge or hatred in them. But, if they were around when their friends were killed and without mercy, I couldn't honestly say."

"But what I can say is when they are threatened they will respond like any trapped animal, but wouldn't any of us? And I don't think for a minute that they had anything to do with the deaths of that family.

"I am curious though what did cause their deaths, and don't tell me you are not curious. Is it not more important to find out that, rather than chasing these them around the countryside?"

Both Karl and Sykes looked at John with astonishment but it was Sykes who questioned John's logic, by asking:

"What would be the outcome if these men walking around the countryside, as you put it, had been in contact with the family? At least with the man because they were the ones that probably buried him. What if they were infected? We can't answer your question yet – as to what they had died of.

"We don't know, the most worrying thing is these men might be carrying whatever it is around unknowing, but I can assure you that it's more than just the common cold."

Karl didn't say a word. He had sat down listening to the banter between John and Sykes.

"I've been thinking along those same lines myself" he said.

"So when you told the media that these men had killed that family, that was untrue?" putting the question to Sykes, who was not to happy to answer.

John could see Karl Ferris was beginning to become impatient with Sykes.

"Would you please tell me why it was deemed necessary to tell everyone?"

"It was thought necessary to warn people not to approach because those men could be dangerous, and if it is infectious we didn't want an epidemic spreading all over the county so the media was brought in just for that reason."

Sykes believed he had skillfully got himself out of the hole he felt he was in. Ferris looked over at Sykes, he couldn't argue with Sykes' logic and in a voice so low John could only just hear what he was saying said:

"Have either of you ever heard the expression 'the media when using all modern technology can be a diabolical weapon for it can warp and corrupt men's minds when it's used to hide the truth'?"

John was impressed. He never imagined for a moment this man would be concerned about what was true and what was a lie.

He soon realised that this man had other things on his mind, which now had him worried. If whatever it was that killed them was that contagious and those men were walking around, and maybe coming into contact with others living nearby, where would it stop?

Margaret and Caroline stood alone away from the rest of the group.

Whatever it was they were discussing they made sure that nobody else heard. Yvonne and the young inspector sat talking about all the things that were happening. Yvonne soon realised it was the inspector that seemed to be doing all the talking, asking questions: how she and John had become involved, what their jobs were and what was expected of them when those men were caught?

There seemed no doubt in the inspector's mind that the fugitives would be caught.

She also asked: "You and John have been inside the zone what are the conditions like inside and did either of you see or speak to any of the men locked away? Do you know what crimes these men had committed?"

"We don't know how we became involved in all of this. We never knew those places ever existed until they told us we were needed to go with them, We are both psychologists and I think they wanted us to assess what use any of these men would be before transferring them to other sites." Yvonne told the policewoman not wishing to hold anything back.

"But I cannot but wonder why such places ever exist, what would justify such a thing? To lock men up and never to let them out, why is it that we have never heard of them before?" asked the young inspector.

"Regarding your question about what crimes those men had committed, that would be a million unit question, does anybody know?"

The young inspector sat back in her chair, thoughts going around in her head, not quite sure what to make of this couple, but not taking her eyes off the woman sitting in front of her for one minute.

Then she decided to ask Yvonne.

"If you truly had not known, or had just put it aside, because I cannot imagine you and John being so connected that you didn't know anything or have at least a inkling what was going on, and what had Sykes meant when he said that they were just machines that talked?"

Yvonne knew what he had meant, but found it hard to find the right words to explain to the young inspector, because she and John had thought it so horrific.

Yet it would be too dangerous to say too much at this stage.

She could not help thinking this young girl was trying to catch her out, so she thought it would be best to play ignorant for now, and see what she says. Inspector Jillian Dove just smiled. She knew what Yvonne had been thinking, but decided not to push it any further for now. She had to be careful just how far she could go before she would be told to drop the case.

To them the deaths of the family and those two men had become the least of their troubles, by the looks on the faces of the three men.

She had also heard of the gangs that roamed the areas outside of the police's jurisdiction, where they lived she had no idea. It would be a good idea to see if she could find out where they are, and speak to some of them to find out if they had seen those men.

Dr Caroline came over and asked the inspector how the police had become involved in the running of work zones, and who gave the permission to investigate because it was nothing to do with them? She pointed out that the zones were private property and said if the policewoman did not drop it she would see that she would be filing in some grimy office for the rest of her time in the force.

Yvonne waited to see what the young inspector's reaction would be to the threat, knowing that if Caroline had the power she could and would carry it out.

Inspector Jillian Dove didn't even take her eyes off her phone, as she punched in another number to whoever it was she was ringing. At first Yvonne thought she had not heard, when she did lift her head, without a word she just handed Caroline her phone and the look on Dr Caroline's face was a picture.

But it didn't last long. When Dr Caroline spoke to the inspector, the tone of her voice was a warning in itself, even Yvonne knew that the young woman had pushed far enough.

The words she spoke confirmed it.

Still the inspector didn't take any notice, but when she spoke her voice was soft and calm, her eyes met Caroline's with confidence, then she started to explain.

"The police have no interest in what happens inside the prison; it's what happens outside is what we are interested in. Those two men that were killed were not in your zone, plus we've now got a dead family. The two cases make it more of a police matter than ever, don't you think?"

"And what I have heard said here today is evidence. If you think that you will be able to cover it up and hide it without having to kill a lot of innocent people you are greatly mistaken."

Yvonne knew that the inspector had probably been referring to the people in the woods that she had spotted when she and John first travelled into Birmingham by train. Was it only a few weeks ago, now it seemed like ages that they had seen them collecting materials from those derelict buildings. There was a time yesterday as they were walking through the woods, when they all knew that they were being watched.

And the young Captain Turner had left them to go find them, returning with a guide.

From the safety of the woods, they would know everything that happened, even what happened at that little farm, and the killing of the two men. Caroline hadn't been involved in the argument between Storrs and the inspector earlier, she had been too busy talking to somebody on the other end of her phone, and now she was talking to someone else but she was not very happy with what she was being told. Then after a while, without a word, she handed Jillian the phone.

When the young inspector handed back the phone she didn't say a word to Caroline.

When she turned to face Yvonne the smile said it all.

# 13

## 13th August

The sun had long gone, now the moon had taken over, bright like a lantern hanging in the sky, covering the tops of the trees with a silver sheet. So after disposing of the corpse of the soldier, the little group of fugitives moved on away from the camp.

Tom had been given the job of escorting the terrified girl up to the stone bridge. Tired and exhausted they had slept a few hours.

It had been their fifth night and today would be their sixth day, far longer than anyone had thought they could survive out in the open.

Their spirits were still high even with the loss of their third member.

They had grown accustomed to the open air and Steve had become quite an accomplished hunter with his new-found toy, the crossbow.

After moving as fast as they could for over three

hours, everyone was ready to drop, but to their surprise it had not been Rose that was beginning to flag but Len, who said: "If I start to hold you back, you must leave me here, out in the open."

Only a gentle breeze helped them from the heat of the mid-morning sun. They were just deciding if it would be safe enough to settle down there in the middle of a field of tall barley when Len, who had dropped behind a little, called for them to come back.

They first thought that he was in trouble, In their haste they had missed a large pipe joining this field to one on the other side of the railway track, allowing access to both fields without having to cross the railway line.

"It would be a perfect place to rest," said Steve. "I'll keep a look out while you can get another couple of hours sleep in peace. It may help Len."

"Steve give me a shake in a hour's time so you can get some sleep as well. How are you feeling Len?" asked Mike. The morning passed over into the afternoon. Steve was quite happy sitting there in the sun, he was used to doing long hours on shifts in the quiet of the night back at the zone.

But by late afternoon he began to feel tired. Taking Mike at his word, he woke Mike they changed places and Steve was soon fast asleep.

Having rested for most of the day the others began to wake up refreshed, Mike warning them not to make too much noise to give Steve a chance for some sleep too.

No one was in too much of a hurry to get going yet,

it was nice and cool in the shade of their new hideout.

At around 17:30 they thought that the end of the world had come.

Everything began to shake, the noise was like nothing on earth.

Steve sat up.

"What on earth's happening?" he exclaimed.

"Don't be too alarmed," said Len. "It's only a train coming along the track. It's going to pass over here any minute now. It may be a little noisy though." The men were reassured.

True to his word, the train passed. It was, as Len predicted, extremely noisy: like a thousand thunderstorms rolled into one.

Reluctant to relinquish their new-found hiding place too quickly, they sat around talking while Jacob produced a warm meal.

By the time everything had been cleared away and they were ready to be on their way, it had started to get dark. This would be their sixth night. They had realised it was much better travelling at night than keep finding somewhere to hide during the day.

Mike went in front to make sure that the way was clear, with a warning to be careful. He kept as close to the edge of the hedgerow as he thought safe without falling into a ditch, but he hadn't realised just how far ahead he had wandered.

He suddenly realised that he was all alone. Coming to a large gap in the hedgerow he waited a second or two to see if there was any sound of the others. It was a clear night and out here in the open countryside the sky was filled with stars, the trees and bushes were again coated with a silver film. Still enjoying his stroll, when he heard a sound a little further along, at first he thought it was one of his companions but soon realised his mistake.

As the figure stepped out of the shadows in front of him, his dark green uniform making a perfect camouflage amongst the shadows, his face covered and hidden by the visor fitted to his helmet.

Before he could shout out any alarm to his friends, Mike was thrown backwards by the impact of the bullets hitting his body. By the time his body had hit the ground he was dead? the fourth member to die. Now the killer moved silently, he had fired three shots in succession, all three had hit their target.

Retracing the dead man's footsteps, he went in the direction of the man's companions.

Before he had stood silently as he had watched his first victim come close enough to have a perfect shot. Now moving silently along the same route that his victim had come, like a hunter going in for the kill, the excitement filling every muscle in his body, fuelled by the adrenaline, not realising that the shots had also warned his would-be victims, and unknown to him, they also were armed.

Steve, who had been out hunting for rabbits with the crossbow, had also heard the gunshots, and had counted how many shots had been fired. He wondered how many more of his friends were dead. Quickly he loaded the crossbow.

The others had not been far behind Mike and had also heard the shots, and had a good idea in which direction the shots had come from.

But their main concern was for their two friends, Mike and Steve, out there in the open. What had happened? Were they both safe? But the lone soldier had also heard their clumsy movements through the trees, and decided to wait hidden well away amongst the bushes, and for them to come into his sights.

Taking off the protective vest and the visor, so he could see more clearly and there would be no fear of any reflections, he stepped back to hide in the shadows of the huge rhododendron bushes that were growing in abundance alongside the lane. Well hidden he waited.

He watched as Leo came out of the bushes into the clearing, not realising that danger was standing just a few metres away.

The soldier smiled as Leo walked into his sights, his finger began to squeeze the trigger.

As Leo had stepped out into the clearing, for a moment his mind had been elsewhere, watching the young rabbits playing amongst the trees, wishing if only he could have been born out here.

He had no idea of the danger he was walking into until the first bullet tore into his body. He had no time to feel any pain, as the second bullet took the top half of his head away.

Pleased at his night's work, the soldier stood hovering over his second victim, gloating over the body, waiting just for one more kill. But he far to confident and eager and it was already too late when he heard the sound of a footstep behind him.

Now the hunter had become the hunted, and with no protective gear. Spinning around in the direction of the sound, he was in Steve's sights, the bolt from Steve's crossbow hit its target, before he could take any defensive action and without any protective vest.

The bolt from Steve's crossbow found it's mark ripping through his chest taking the man's lungs and heart with it.

Seconds before he died he felt the pain and realised that he had paid the price for being over-confident and gloating over his two victims.

When, and only when they were sure he was dead, did they emerge out from their hiding places to see if their friends were still alive or dead. It did not take them long to discover the bodies. Mike was the fourth and Leo the fifth of the eleven that had escaped, so now there were only six of them plus the girl.

Bringing the two bodies together Tom and Jim began to dig a shallow hole big enough for both, so they would be together always. Covering the bodies with soil and stones, that they collected from under the trees, to stop any wild animals disturbing the grave.

Tom made a little cross out of a couple of branches and placed it on top of the grave. Jim, Steve and Ken watched in silence over the grave while Tom read a few lines from his little red book.

Taking the man's ammunition which matched

his own, then handing it to Jim who, under Steve's instructions, checked just how much ammunition the weapons magazine was left.

Seeing that there was only a few rounds left, he took the weapon and threw it as far he could amongst the trees.

They decided to return to where Rose and Jacob had been left for their safety and to take care of Len, who for the last few hours had been complaining about ache's in his joints and muscles.

Jacob had checked that they had everything that they would need and they were getting ready to leave.

They had heard the shots and it had been over an hour since they heard anything from them. They were getting a little worried and Rose seemed to be concerned about Len's condition.

She had been told to say, if they were caught before they got back, that she had been forced and brought here against her will, and not to worry too much about Len, he would not suffer.

By the time the four of them walked into the little camp, it had been over two hours, checking their watches they could see that it was well past midnight. Rose went straight to Tom flinging her arms around his neck, the others just looked at each other and smiled. They had noticed that there was some kind of bond building up between the two of them, similar to that of Mark and Phil. Holding Rose so close Tom could feel a longing sweep through his whole body, he could not remember ever feeling like this in his whole life. It was strange, but a feeling of disappointment swept over his body when she pulled away from him.

The look of bewilderment on her face, Tom could not understand why, but she had just realised that there were two of the group missing.

After it had been explained to Rose through hand signs, and to Jacob, Len what had happened to Mike and Leo and the killing of the guard, they sat down to rest and have something to eat while they thought about the friends they had lost, in silence. Rose, with hand signs, said that she was sorry for the two that had died, but she was happy that Tom had returned back safely.

The last time they had eaten was hours ago.

This would be the morning of their seventh day out in the open. The skies looked like there could be a shower or two. The clouds had been gathering for most of the morning.

They had been on the move most of the night, and by the time they had finished the meal, it would soon be dawn. Time now for a few hours sleep. While the rest tried to get some sleep, Jim and Steve discussed what they should do the next day, or where to go. They soon realised that they didn't have a clue where they were.

Later that morning, just before the sun had risen over the tree tops, they woke to find Ken, who had been up and about for quite a while.

"I've been having a look around and I've seen an old signpost further along the towpath," he said. "It's partly rotted away with age. It points two ways: the first to Lapworth; the second to a place called Packwood.

"I've had a quick walkabout. There's a small lane leading down to Packwood. It looks like a large private house with its own grounds. I think we ought to stay clear."

Taking out the old map, which Len had handed over also a little object in a box, he placed the map on the ground, then waited for the others to gather round. And with a little help from Len, he pointed out the precise position where they were to the amazement of the others he had been a quick learner.

Then they realised he and Len had been tracking all their movements on the map. He produced out of his pocket the object, which they didn't recognise or have any idea what it's purpose was.

"It's a compass, Len found it at the house" he said. "I've marked all the paths and canals and the names of the roads that we've crossed since our escape."

Len came over and after a few seconds studying the map, he began to move his finger along a line on the map. The others thought it to be nothing more than a crease in the paper, but he patiently pointed out to them all the roads, rivers, railways and spider's web of canals.

"How do you know all this?" asked Jim.

"Don't you think me and Ken had enough time to study these things?" replied Len.

His finger continued to follow the line, then stopped at a spot on the map, explaining to the others exactly where the canals met.

"And this is Lapworth" said Ken It's about a hour's walk from here if we keep to the path, but if we carry on over the fields it maybe a little longer, I should think."

He left his finger on the spot; with another he pointed to elsewhere.

"This is where we've escaped from," he said. "It's taken us six days; it's not all that far but because of all the criss-crossing that we've done we've covered quite a distance in real terms."

What he had not told them was that he hadn't been feeling too good himself the last few hours.

"I've been thinking," said Jim. "We shouldn't worry too much about those chasing us because I don't think they'll bother to follow us. All they'll do is form a circle round the area and wait for us to appear."

He had been accepted as the leader because of the one chance remark (that none could remember). But Jim had made their dream come true by organising the escape. If they had any idea what he'd risked for a taste of walking freely in the open air.

Even now, with five of their friends dead, there were no regrets. They all knew what the outcome would be, right from the start.

"Have any of you noticed", asked Steve, "that we haven't heard the dogs barking for the last couple of nights?"

He knew how the authorities worked? as did Jim.

"What do you suggest we do?" asked Tom.

"Because if they're just waiting for us, where can we go?"

No-one answered immediately.

"We should head for Lapworth," said Ken after a few moments thought.

"It's where the canals meet. They moor the boats there. We've seen them travelling up and down the canals. Maybe there's an unused one.

"We could borrow it for a while. If we're lucky, we'll slip through unnoticed.

"They aren't going to stop every one of them, surely?"

Jacob looked up from packing away his cooking pots.

"Well it's not going to be for long, is it?" he said.

He then burst out laughing.

It was the very first time in their lives they had heard the sound of real laughter, then every one of them could not help but see the funny side of Jacobs remark and joined in the laughter.

Leaving the rest in good humour, Steve and Jim went off to see if the way was clear, while the rest of them finished getting the bags packed before it started to rain.

Tom had been given the task of looking after Rose, he was to get her away no matter what happened to the rest of them. They all felt that they had a duty to protect her since they had put her in this predicament. He still could not help thinking of Mark, Phil, Joe, Mike and Leo.

Seeing Tom so sad, Rose came and sat down by his side, then without any warning she took his hand in hers, bringing it to her lips she gave it a gentle kiss. Jacob, who had been watching, just smiled.

"I wonder if there are any more guards waiting for us to appear?" asked Jim as he and Steve walked along the towpath. They had slept most of the day in a hollow covered by the hedgerow that ran alongside a narrow lane separating the lane from the canal. By the time they were on the move it had been early evening, the sun low in the sky this would be their seventh night.

They could see that the clouds were gathering with the promise of rain later that night, and the wind had begun to build up and to sweep through the branches, bending some of the young trees until they were touching the ground.

By the time the two of them had got back, everything had been packed away, even the cans that Jacob had found in cupboards at the house, and the vegetables and fruit that they had found in the garden.

"I reckon there should be enough to last another fourteen days or so. We should be OK," Jacob joked.

"Do you really think that we're going to last that long?" asked Ken.

Jacob thought for a moment.

"No, but we still have enough food."

With everything equally shared into each of their bags, they headed off in the direction of Lapworth, not knowing what to expect once they were there. They just hoped that they could retreat (into one of the narrowboats) out of the wind and rain.

"There is one problem, even if there is one that we can get into? which one of us knows anything about them?" asked Jim.

Now it had started to rain quite heavily, and with it being blown into their faces it was hard going, but their thoughts were on Jim's question too much to worry about the weather.

Deciding that it was not worth going on any further, luck was again on their side as just a little further on they found an old barn, still warmed up by its last occupants. There they could take cover from the wind and rain at least till the rain gave over a little.

By the time the rain had passed, it was getting late. It would be better to get away from here, not knowing if or when anyone would be back.

They had been going for three or four hours, their seventh day on the run was drawing to a end.

They came across a strange looking building. It was a funny shape and there seemed to be no walls like the others that they had seen. The roof seemed to curve right down to the ground. The four windows, two on each side, were fitted on this strange roof and at the very top the silhouette of a chimney with just a faint whisper of smoke reaching for the heavens.

The smoke told them that this dwelling was lived in, so they had to be very quiet as not to disturb the occupants.

When they got closer, they could see there was a brick extension built at one end of the building covering quite a bit of ground. Everything was in darkness, nothing moved, even the hens, in their henhouse, were still asleep.

The building was just the width of the towpath away from the canal, where they could see a narrowboat looking a little smaller than the others they had seen before. It was tied up opposite the house.

Checking his watch, Steve could see that it was still only twenty minutes till midnight, so quite early.

"I think we had better leave it for a while to make sure the occupants of the house are fast asleep," he said.

# 14

John stood by the door studying the map hanging on the wall. It was the very same one that had attracted him the very first time they had come through these doors.

The painting that had covered it before had been removed.

John still wanted to know what was the significance of the different coloured pegs on the map and he was still trying to guess what each colour represented when he was joined by Yvonne, his wife, and Jillian Dove, the young police inspector. Neither of them could answer John's problem, they were just as puzzled as he was.

Still pondering over the significance of some and guessing others, they were joined by the Director of Production, Mark Sykes, who they had grown to know quite well over the last few weeks? he a little too sure of himself for Yvonne's liking.

She also thought that he must live a very good life: he was a little overweight and he also wore too much eau de cologne, the fragrance lingered over him like a cloud they could smell him as he approached.

But his smile was a plus and counteracted all his minuses, and when he spoke his voice would soften any woman's heart.

Talking softly his manners were impeccable. He was a gentleman and soon won the two women over and, beckoning John to come closer, he began to explain all the significant colours on the board. Some they had already guessed, the blue they had already been told were the machine areas, like the one where they were before being called here.

But when he came to explain the significance of the flag coloured pink, it made all three even angrier. Like all the other zones it was for production, but this was for the production of children.

They could feel each other's disgust at what they had just heard, made worse by the way he had said it, so smug. John felt like he could have hit the man. Sykes must have guessed what they had been thinking, his voice was still soft as he said:

"Before you start letting off steam let me explain something.

"Two centuries ago something happened, what it was no one seems to know exactly, but then the population of the world was much greater than it is now, by how much we have no idea, nor do we know what happened. But we have been told the world was over-populated."

He stopped to have a sip of the drink he had been holding, and to let them digest what they had learnt.

Placing his empty glass on a ledge under the map he continued.

"It was so bad that certain areas were overcrowded to the extent that food, water and fuel were on the point of running out.

"All we do know is that something terrible happened and for several years after, there were not enough people to fulfil all the work, to make a fresh start and to make all those things that we would require to exist."

He stopped again as the rest of the room gathered around intrigued, while someone fetched chairs for the women.

Sykes went to get another drink, and when everyone was seated he continued.

"And the only places that seemed not to be affected as bad were the prisons. So the prisons were converted into work zones, each man was trained in the trades, but as they grew old and died, other ways had to be thought of. To build robotic machines was out, there was no-one to build them, plus there were no materials to build them with. Luckily a few years before, the prisoners sperm had been collected while they were still quite young men, and then frozen."

"Now I know what you meant when you referred to them as just machines that talk," said John.

"What about the pink pins?" asked Yvonne. "Do they stand for what I think they do?"

Sykes gave a sly smile and nodded. "They are the maternity zones for the surrogate mothers. At first they were meant to supply only the work force, but as you know full well, most of the women now have careers and do not want the pain or inconvenience of looking after their own child. "But they do want to be mothers and have families, so now most choose to use the surrogate mothers.

"So you see they had no choice, it was a case of eat our morals or for civilisation to wither and die," added Sykes, continuing to defend past deeds. "Inspector you only have to see that the laws are upheld, you haven't got the dirty job of making those sometime dirty laws," Margaret Storrs said, looking at the inspector, warning her to be careful.

Yvonne could not disagree. Most of the people that she knew had used the service at least once. They were joined by a young man who came over and stood by the side of Margaret Storrs's chair, and whispered something into her ear. He gave the inspector a look that warned her something was wrong.

When the director did speak her voice was stern informing them:

"Three bodies have been found. One was one of us, the second was a escapee, the third was the boy who had been missing. He had been attacked from behind and thrown into the lock with his pockets packed with stones. So inspector, what is your answer to that?"

The young inspector had no answer, only to let Storrs know that if that was the case, then they must be brought to trial. But the threat fell on deaf ears because Margaret Storrs knew she would have the backing of those much higher than this young pipsqueak.

"Don't you think inspector, that if any of my guards came across these murderers, that they wouldn't shoot to kill?" Sykes interjected.

"Those men, out there, on the run... they're very dangerous. On the grounds of public safety inspector, would you, honestly, take the rap if any more innocent people were killed, just because you thought they must have a trial? You forget... these are just talking machines. They don't come under the law of the land."

"They aren't talking machines just because you say so or it's for our benefit," replied the inspector. "I'll tell you all here right now, that if anyone, and I mean anyone, is killed, there'll be an investigation. And that comes from the highest court in the land. I wasn't stupid enough to come here without doing my homework first."

The young inspector could barely disguise the disdain in her voice.

"Oh... there's one more thing," she added. "If anyone's interested... I read about a King who once thought he was above the law. Poor fellow lost his head."

John and Yvonne said nothing, for there was nothing they could say.

They knew nothing about the legislation and didn't want to get the young woman into any more trouble. Even so, they felt a little uneasy at what they'd just heard.

Karl Ferris had been sitting silently listening to the argument between the three. But now he thought it was time to say something, his tone of voice had hardened.

"My dear young lady," he said, patronisingly. "Don't come in here threatening us. You do your job and we'll do ours."

He then turned to face Sykes.

"Haven't you been listening to me? We must stop thinking of these men as talking machines because, up till now, they've got the better us."

Margaret Storrs and the inspector were still arguing about the ethics when the huge door opened. One of the guards entered and went directly to Margaret. He spoke so quietly that no-one else knew what was being said. Upon finishing, Margaret braced herself to face the others.

"The orders are," she said, "to shoot on sight."

The look on Detective Inspector Jillian Dove's face was a picture. She was determined not to let them think they could just please themselves about what laws to follow and what laws they chose to ignore.

"If your men feel that they or any of the public are in danger," she said.

"They're well within their rights to use as much force as they deem necessary."

"Thank you, inspector, for explaining that", said Ferris. "Now, can we get on with the business in hand and capture these men?"

The smile on his face fooled no-one.

One hour later, they were all travelling towards the Work Zone including, and against Margaret Storrs' express wishes, Jillian Dove.

Margaret had no time for the young inspector. She

believed that those with power could make and break the rules as they think fit.

On the journey back to the zone, Inspector Dove turned to face Margaret and asked her:

"There's something puzzling me," she said. "Maybe you could help?" Margaret listened attentively.

"What would happen if, say, these fugitives meet someone who befriends them? What happens then? To that person, I mean?" Margaret smirked.

"They couldn't be charged for aiding and abetting criminals," continued the inspector, "because, as far as the law of the land's concerned, they've committed no crime."

"What about that young boy and the soldier?" asked Ferris.

He was losing patience with the inspector.

"I don't know the circumstances of the boy's death, so I can't comment on that. What I will say, though... if any one of us, in this vehicle, were to have a gun to our face, wouldn't we protect ourselves?"

Without uttering another word, she turned to face the window, and watched as the trees and fields flew past.

No-one else said a word until the vehicle pulled up outside the gates of the Work Zone.

Captain Turner was there to meet them with the news that another soldier's body had been found along with the bodies of another two fugitives.

"So that means six of 'em are still out there", said Sykes. "What are you doing about it, Captain?"

It was the first time he'd spoken since leaving the

council offices. "Well sir, as you already know… we've placed a cordon round the area and are slowly closing in on the fugitives."

The captain sounded a little nervous.

Yvonne thought that maybe he was thinking that he could end up being the scapegoat for the arrogance of the others.

"How many men do you have, Captain?" asked Ferris.

"Twenty of my own and Margaret's fifty … making a total of seventy, sir."

"We can add up for ourselves, Captain," replied Margaret Storrs acidly.

"Do you think that'll be enough men for the job?" remarked Ferris.

His voice remained calm.

"I think so, because if there are too many of us roaming around, don't you think the general public would start to ask questions?" said the captain.

He wanted to ensure that he wasn't going to take the blame if anything went wrong. He remembered the time when they first met and he'd been ignored.

Ferris turned to the captain.

"I'd like to go and see for myself where these men are hiding", said the former. "I don't know why they haven't been caught yet. What is it? Seven days now?"

"It's getting late. Wouldn't you prefer to leave it till tomorrow morning – as by the time we got there, it'd be getting dark?" said the captain, "unless you fancy a night under the stars?"

They all smiled at the young captain's attempt at sarcasm. Even Margaret and Dr Caroline smiled.

"My dear Captain, has no-one ever told you that sarcasm's the lowest form of wit?" Karl Ferris said with a smile, signalling to all in the room that no offence had been taken.

"But you are right Captain. I have heard that there maybe more than just humans roaming around those woods, so I don't think any of us would fancy camping out there tonight, let alone these beautiful women."

With a little bow of his head, and a sweep of his hand in the direction of the four women, Ferris lent back into his chair.

By the time everyone had finished their meal, and their fair share of drinks, it was getting late.

So when he suggested that they should be thinking of having an early night because he intended to make a early start, they all began to make their way to their rooms.

When everyone else had left, John and Yvonne wanted to stay up a while longer, to discuss all that they had learnt over the past weeks.

Through no fault of their own, they felt that they had got mixed up in something they had no control over, and had no idea what it was or how to get out of it.

Early next morning they were out on the road, heading for the area where the bodies of the soldier and the two fugitives were found.

Eight days the fugitives had been on the run, those in London were not very happy. This was going on for far too long, questions had started to be asked. The young captain had agreed with Karl, they wanted to be on the road as soon as possible because they had been informed that the area where they would be going was sometimes very busy with the narrowboats going to and forth. And he didn't want any more of his men, or anyone getting mixed up if there is any trouble and getting themselves killed.

# 15

Along the canal, when the moon broke free of the clouds, they could see in the near distance some more locks, then further down they could see more, and opposite there were lines of boats moored? all tied up alongside each other. They were in darkness so if they were occupied, then the occupants were still fast asleep.

Turning their attention back to the dwelling they could still see a whisper of smoke coming from the chimney, yet the morning was quite warm so who on earth would anyone want a fire?

Deciding that it was time to move, it had just turned 04:30, it was now or never to see if the boat tied up nearest them was unlocked or they could get into it without waking everyone in the area up. This would be their eighth day, if only they could make it.

Now as they came closer, something else had caught their attention. One of the hatches on the side nearest the towpath was slightly open, so it may be possible for one of them to climb in.

The question was who, and could it be Len, who said

he had read and understood a little about the narrowboats, but he had been ill for the last two days? Would he or any of them be able to handle such a monster?

When they asked him if he thought he could handle one, Len said: "I think I should be able to," sounding a little more sure of himself than he was.

He had not been feeling too well since they had left that house.

He was above normal height but very thin, and said he would feel a little better after a rest; he would try and get in and start the monster up while they untied the ropes.

Even though it had only been seven days in the open, they were all getting quite tanned, and Jacob started to jest on several occasions that they would soon be the same colour as himself.

For the first time in their lives they all knew what it felt like to be happy, even if tomorrow, one or even all of them, may be dead, they had no regrets. They had accomplished what they had wanted, to see what it was like beyond those wall's. They liked what they had seen.

As they approached they could see that the boat was much smaller than the ones that they had seen going along the canals. Len stepped down onto the stern, before slowly making his way along the side of the boat checking the hatches as he went, until he came across the one that wasn't locked. After looking inside and seeing that it was vacant he climbed inside. Taking a few steps along a narrow passage, he soon came upon the hatch leading on to the stern sheets.

After a few minutes checking over the controls, he had worked on different machines all his life, this was no problem. When he turned the key that he had found on the table just inside the cabin, as the engine burst into life, he shouted for the others to jump on board.

Even though they couldn't hear him over the noise, they soon jumped on board when they saw the propellers begin to turn and the little boat started pulling against its mooring they hadn't had time to release it.

The engine had only run a short time but the noise had been enough to wake the occupants of the house. As the door swung open, an old man stepped out into the open air pointing an ancient shotgun in their direction.

He shouted for them to get off their boat and stand still, or he would shoot the first man that does not obey.

Moving away from the doorway to get a better look at those who were attempting to steal his boat, and as he stepped forwards another figure followed.

The companions looked on in astonishment.

How old were these people? They had never seen anyone looking so old. Finding it hard not to burst out laughing, as the old man came up closer he looked even older, his face and hands were like tanned leather and covered in wrinkles, but he held the gun steady.

Tom felt the barrel of the ancient gun being pressed into his stomach and he had been convinced it would be very unwise of him not to take this old man seriously.

Speaking to no-one in particular he asked: "Are you the ones that had escaped from the prison?"

There was a look in his eyes and a sound in his voice of a wise and fair man. Before he or anyone could say anything, Steve stepped out of the shadows where he had been standing, aiming the deadly crossbow in the direction of the old couple, instructing the man to put the gun down.

Stepping back the man positioned himself between Steve and the woman who had come from the safety of the house to be with her husband. In her hand she had a rather lethal looking knife, both stood firm wanting to protect their property from the strangers.

When he spoke it was as a young man, even more defiant than ever saying:

"If you intend to kill me and my wife it will be at a price."

Slowly he guided his wife back towards the open doorway.

"We do not intend to harm you, all we want to do is see what the outside world was like before we die. You are quite safe, we were just looking at the boat," Tom said, desperately trying to calm things down and explain the reason why they were gathered outside their property.

"Why?" said the old man. "Are you thinking of hiring it?"

Tom noted another tone in the man's voice. This time the man seemed to be jesting with them as he smiled.

"What do you mean by hire?" Tom asked.

Now it was the woman's turn to explain.

"We mean... that for the time that you borrow the boat, you give us money or units from your credit."

The fugitives all looked at one another in bewilderment, not having the slightest idea what money, credit or units were.

The only one to understand what she meant was Jacob, who said to the woman:

"We have neither money nor credit, but we are willing to do any work that needs doing for the loan of your boat."

"How long do you want it for?" asked the old man. The woman turning to her husband told him not to ask such a question.

"Don't ask that dear," she said, and they could tell by the softness in her voice she understood that their life expectancy was not to be measured in weeks or even days, then the man also understood.

Then with a nod, he indicated for them to follow, nestling the gun in his arms like a baby. He turned to go back into the house, followed by his wife, with the seven of them following close behind.

It wasn't until everyone was inside and in the light that both the man and woman, realised that one of the group was a girl, giving Rose a closer look, the woman with a degree of concern.

She asked: "Are you alright my dear, haven't I seen you up at the big house when I took some vegetables up the other week? Weren't you one of servant girls?"

Rose tried with hand signals to explain the circumstances of her being with the group. After a few minutes, the woman nodded.

Jim noticed that Len wasn't there with them. He looked around.

"Has anyone seen Len?" he asked.

Everyone looked at each other.

"I think he's still on the boat," said Ken. "I didn't see him come off, and he's been feeling bad the last few days. He's been really sick today. I don't think he's been eating all that well either."

"And how do you feel?" asked Jim.

"Not too bad," said Ken, "but I've been sick a couple of times."

Not wanting to worry the old couple, they all went back outside to find Len. They found him lying on one of the seats in the boats cabin, lying still with his head in his arms. At first they thought that he was just asleep.

Steve climbed down into the dark cabin to see if he was alright, concerned when Len didn't even stir as he approached. He decided to check his pulse and soon realised that another of their friends was dead. Had he died of the same thing that had killed the family? If so, what could it be? And what about poor Ken? He was also feeling sick. Together both Len and Ken had buried the man at the farm.

Tom noticed a piece of paper lying on the table, when he picked it up Tom realised Len, knowing that he was dying, had drawn a rough map of the canals and noted the places that they had passed through.

So now they had a boat and a map, so maybe it would be possible to keep their promise.

Steve picked up the body of his friend as if it didn't weigh a thing, and carried it ashore to a little garden by the edge of path. It was filled with geraniums, lobelia of different colours, three or four climbing roses, climbed up the front of the house filling the air with a beautiful aroma supported by thin wires fixed to the wall.

The woman told them to lay the body on the garden amongst the flowers, not on the hard path, explaining that it will be safe there until the soldiers came. Another member of the party had now died.

Dawn would be soon upon them and, again, the canals would be busy.

Leaving their dead friend amongst the flowers, they all returned inside.

Jacob who had stayed inside, he was busy in the kitchen sorting something out for breakfast.

"I would like to cook something for you both before we leave, that's if you don't mind?" I'm a chef he said to the woman.

"It'll be nice to have someone else do the cooking for a change," she said.

The woman said her name as Mary; and her husband's Brian.

While she and Jacob were busy preparing the food, the man had taken the rest around the house.

Steve said to the man; "I don't think that those coming after us will be here till much later in the day, so if there's anything you need doing just say. We can fix most things: any lifting, cutting any wood that you need cutting."

So after a few hours a pile of wood had been cut and stored away, and the few repairs that had needed to be done around the house had been done, even the garden had been tidied up.

Sitting by the canal enjoying the morning sun the old man made sure all the passing boats saw him, and stopped to chat.

They told him about the escaped convicts and that the police had cordoned off the area.

The old man asked one of the skippers:

"Are the police coming to see if we're OK?"

"Not yet," came the skipper's reply. They seemed to be to busy.

Steve, who had been on board their boat with Ken, had been listening to everything that had been said, and knew that he had been right to say they would not be in too much of a hurry to move in, especially if they had found the bodies.

But now it was time for them to be on the move.

Their intention was to be well away from here, in case one of the narrowboats had spotted and reported the activity around the old lock keeper's house. They didn't want to get the couple into any trouble and be asked too many difficult questions.

Jim had suggested that it would be a good Idea to tie the pair of them up, then they could just say we forced them.

Thinking it was a good idea, the couple agreed.

Jacob said: "I have spoken to Brian and Mary and they have said they would like it if I would stay and help them as they're both getting old. I would be handy around the house and the locks."

They asked Rose if she would like to stay but Rose said:

"I'd like to go wherever Tom goes."

Jim and Tom asked the couple if they realised the dangers they would be putting themselves in if the authorities recognised Jacob.

The man didn't answer, just gave a that look which told Tom that he and his wife knew full well what the consequences were, yet it didn't deter them. Before they left, the three would be tied up? but not too tightly, just enough to make it plausible.

The old man had given them a quick run through the running of his pride and joy, his narrowboat, and showed them how to work the locks.

Saying their goodbyes to the old couple and Jacob was one of the saddest things the five had felt. Even in that short time, a kind of friendship had been built up.

As the boat went on its way, the five stood in the stern looking back at the house, hoping that they had done the right thing by leaving Jacob alone with the couple.

Would they just turn him over to the authorities when they arrived?

Would they be safe?

A feeling of remorse fell over the crew. Out of the eleven that had escaped only four remained.

They were on their way. At first, it took time to get used to the steering of the boat in and out of the locks but, after a while, it became much easier, each taking their turn.

After spending most of their eighth day at the lock

keeper's house, they would soon have to start looking out for somewhere to tie up for the night.

With the sun still out, and with the steady speed of eight knots, it had turned out to be a pleasant evening. Steve had been doing most of the steering while Tom and Jim took it in turns to do the locks.

Every so often Ken spotted another boat coming the other way. With Steve steering, Ken in the bows, and the other three hiding in the cabin below, they would pass as just another working boat.

It was still early evening when they came to a place where the canal widened.

They decided to tie up for the night before it was too dark. After making sure the boat was well secured, the five decided to take a walk along the edge of the canal by a field where the wheat was nearly as high as them, golden brown, ready for harvesting.

It was a beautiful evening. Across the fields they could see cattle waiting to be milked; in the field opposite, tractors collecting in the year's harvest.

Listening to the birds singing in the trees as they walked along the canal-edge, they were beginning to feel much better. Out here, they could forget everything.

Back on board they ate what Jacob had prepared for them, then turned in for the night.

Their eighth day had come to an end.

Tomorrow would be their ninth day of freedom.

Day nine.

They had never seen or felt anything so peaceful. The early morning sun poured through the open hatches.

They had awoken quite late, and as they wanted to be on the move before anyone started to ask them awkward questions, they had to make do with just a bite to eat before going on their way.

Travelling slowly, with Steve at the wheel, the others lounged about on the roof of the cabin, enjoying the sun. Ken kept watch in the bows. He wore old clothes that had been given to him by the old man. Keeping watch wasn't too demanding, although he'd felt quite ill for some time.

The rest were getting worried, especially after what had happened to Len. Steve told them all to be ready to get over the side as quick as they could if their pursuers were spotted, or they were stopped.

It wasn't long before a lone soldier was spotted? who signalled for them to pull over to the side. Steve, who was also wearing some old overalls and an old flat cap that he had acquired off one of the other boats, taking his time to respond to the command, wanting to give the others time to slip over the side into the dirty water and to hide amongst the reeds on the opposite bank, keeping them hidden from view by the boat, leaving just himself and Ken on board.

As the boat pulled alongside the soldier jumped on board, holding the automatic weapon as if it were a baby cradled across his arm, he was ready for any trouble.

Ken had been watching the soldier as he come on board, from where he sat hiding in the bows, not daring to open his mouth.

Steve seemed to take all the questioning quite calmly.

Tom, Jim and Rose, hiding amongst the tall bulrushes, watched everything that was going on from a safe distance. All seemed to be going fine until the soldier was joined by another, who seemed to be the man's superior.

All of a sudden the second soldier turned his gun towards Steve's chest as the first man disappeared into the cabin to search inside, while Ken, who had been given a signal from Steve, began to slowly and quietly slip over the side and lower himself into the icy water.

He had just made the cover of the reeds when the original soldier returned from below, carrying the crossbow and began asking Steve more questions.

Demanding to speak to the man that was in the bows, and when they were not able to find him, that was when the commotion broke out, on board.

Those hiding among the reeds watched as the pantomime began to play out its course on board.

Just one single shot broke the silence of the morning.

Steve fell backwards over the side into the dirty water.

He wasn't dead, just wounded. He began to swim towards the opposite shore just as Ken was about to break his cover and go back to help his friend. The soldier, realising the swimming man had only been wounded, let off a burst from his automatic gun, covering the water with deadly pieces of lead, with several finding their intended target. The water surrounding Steve began to turn scarlet, blood pouring out of the many wounds.

Rose who had never seen anyone die so tragically

couldn't hold back the tears. Steve, like the rest, had become a good friend; she felt that for once in her short life this little group were the only ones that she could depend on.

Ken had joined them as they watched the two soldiers struggling to haul Steve's body out of the water and onto the deck of the boat.

It was the one thing in their favour. The soldiers were too pre-occupied to look for them, so this was their chance to get going before the soldiers were joined by others, or decided to look in their direction.

Moving slowly through the reeds for a further three hundred metres in the cold water, further along the water's edge where it was overlapped by branches of a small copse of young trees. The bank of the canal had collapsed into the water. so this would be the ideal place to crawl out of the freezing water, hopefully unseen.

Lying amongst the branches and undergrowth, Tom, Jim, Ken and Rose watched as another group made their way along the opposite path to join the two soldiers still on board.

Tom recognised them. They were the one's that had visited the zone a few weeks earlier, especially the one woman with red hair and green eyes. There was something about her that spelled trouble.

Another of the group, a woman, stood out even more so. She was petite with tight curly hair. It was she who Tom remembered had spotted him on the roof. She had stopped to look and seemed to be able to read his every thought, but had not said a word.

He said: "Does anyone else remember any one of that group?"

Jim said that he remembered all of them; he had been informed that they were VIPs sent from central government, but no-one seemed to be sure for what purpose.

Watching from their hideout, the four decided it was their chance to quickly slip away, but realised that the only way was to go back into the water amongst the reeds where they could move without being seen. They gently lowered themselves back into the freezing water not wanting to attract any attention to themselves. They moved slowly, up to their necks In the icy water, even submerging completely when there was a break between the reeds.

Jim led the way while Tom looked after Rose, helping her along as best as he could; Ken followed behind, like Len he also had not complained through they knew he had not been feeling too good the last two days. Jim asked Tom to keep an eye on him.

Tom had noticed that Jim had become withdrawn since Len's death, blaming himself for all their friends' deaths, his concern for Ken was even more so since Len's death.

After navigating along the banks of the canal for another twenty minutes, they reached a bend in the canal, putting themselves out of sight of those swarming over the boat like bees over a pot of honey.

High above their heads, about ten or so metres, and spanning the canal was what looked like another bridge, but this was different: this one was made of metal.

Jim, Tom and Rose had been so pre-occupied in the bridge that it was only when they'd they pulled themselves onto the bank, freezing and soaking wet, did they realise that Ken wasn't with them.

Jim and Tom dropped bank into the water and retraced their route back, even at the risk of been spotted by those on the opposite bank, they had to go and see if he needed any help. They found him just a few metres back lying face down amongst the reeds. He had not called out for help for fear that those on the opposite bank would hear. He had died tangled amongst the reeds in the cold icy water.

Twenty minutes later, the two men pulled their friend's body onto dry land into a clearing, well away from the reeds that had clung around his body. They wanted to be sure that he would be found, before any animals gnawed away at his body.

Because if there was one thing this experience had taught them, it was compassion. They felt a little guilty at the loss of all their friends, even though it had been for only for a short time, they had enjoyed and valued the freedom.

On the boat the search was over. They had recovered Steve's body out of the water while some of the soldiers ran along the towpath towards the little lock keeper's house on the side of the canal, where they had been informed there had been sightings of the men.

The soldiers ran as fast as they could to check if all the occupants were safe. Reaching the house Len's body was soon discovered lying amongst the flowers of the small rose garden, but before the body was allowed to be taken away Dr Caroline wanted to have a closer look. There was something different about this one. There were no wounds or marks apart from those on his torso. She'd seen similar such marks, not too long ago, at the farm.

Minutes later, both the old man and woman were released. Jacob, however, was left as he'd been found, even though the old man and woman had sworn that he'd been their hired hand for the past couple of years.

But after they had explained to Margaret Storrs and Caroline that the woman had been very ill and the old man had said that he would not be able to look after her but for Jacob, he was released and he quickly made himself scarce in case someone began to get suspicious.

He knew one of the women was, he had heard one of the men call her Yvonne.

She and the man with her kept looking over in his direction, as if he was trying to remember where he had seen him before.

Jacob remembered them all from when they had first visited the Work Zone, but now all he could hope for was that they didn't remember him.

# 16

Yvonne had recognised Jacob. She knew that she had seen him working in the kitchens but wasn't sure if she should say anything because she wasn't quite sure what would happen to the old couple if Margaret thought that they had helped the prisoners.

Also the old couple seemed to be dependent on him, especially at their age. Yvonne thought it would be criminal to deprive them of their helper, so she said nothing.

Margaret came through into the kitchen telling everybody: "Get ready to be on the move, we now know that they have a boat,

"Also the girl is with them and we know she is with them of her own free will, so now she is also *Beyond Salvage* and so must be shot on sight."

Within half an hour a dozen or so heavily armed soldiers moved off in the direction they had come, after realising that the remaining escapees were heading back in the direction they had started from.

What they couldn't understand is why on earth were they heading back? What were they up to?

Surely they must realise the whole area was swarming with people, everyone looking for them and there was nowhere for them to go.

Moving swiftly the little group followed in the same direction as the soldiers, Captain Turner telling the sergeant that if they were heading back towards the zone, to make sure they would be ready for them when they arrived. There was one thing that worried him, he had no idea whereabouts on the perimeter they would turn up. The fence covered a large area which would take a lot more men than they had to cover every bit of fence.

All of a sudden from across the other side of the canal, a man that had been walking his dog, called out, attracting their attention, which he certainly had. Some of the soldiers were shouting back, asking him to explain what all the noise was about. The man standing on the opposite bank just pointed at the ground but no-one could make out what it was that he was pointing at. Under the instructions of Captain Turner, they began to swing the bows of the boat around so that it so it spanned the canal forming a bridge.

When the temporary bridge was complete, several of the soldiers rushed over to where man and his dog stood. He was standing near what looked just like a pile of old rags, maybe left there by one of the passing boats.

Only when they were standing close to the pile of rags did it become clear that it was another body.

They were still trying to decide what to do when Captain Turner arrived, wanting to know if this was one of the escapees or some innocent bypasser. The man with the dog made some excuse and left them to decide what they should do with the body.

They were still discussing what to do when they were joined by DrCaroline.

There had been a significant change in her over the last few days, ever since they had come across all those graves of the poor children and the family. She didn't have any children of her own, not even choosing to go through the official channels of the surrogate zones. She'd put her career first but, over the last couple of days, she couldn't stop wondering if she'd made a terrible mistake. Even when she thought of the bodies lying there, she was piqued that the children had died together. She had no-one to mourn her or indeed, anyone to remember her, only Margaret. Even then, sometimes, while she lay in bed, she would wonder just how long the memories would last.

She watched as the soldiers began to manhandle the body, shouting at them to be careful. They still hadn't decided if this was one of the escapees or not. She then ordered that both bodies be put with the other one that they had found back at the lock-keeper's house, and the three must be taken back to the morgue?where she could carry out a post-mortem.

She was concerned now as to the cause of their deaths, watching closely to make sure that they lifted Ken's body gently.

She couldn't stop thinking about the family and what had caused their deaths. The desecration of the man's body could be put down to wild animals, rats? But what about the rest of the family?

She entertained the idea to have the graves of the family exhumed and the bodies taken, along with the bodies of the three fugitives, to the morgue. Any idea that the cause of the deaths of these three men could be the same as the family began to trouble her.

What if the man that had been shot, in the water, also showed signs? What then?

Margaret Storrs, who had chosen to stay behind with the others, was joined by Karl Ferris and the young policewoman, Jillian Dove – who was talking to John and Yvonne Dampier (the husband and wife team of Psychoanalysts.)

Ferris was busy looking through a pair of binoculars trying to find out where the remaining fugitives were heading.

He couldn't even see them. "Where on earth are they?" he asked, to no-one in particular.

Only Captain Turner replied.

"What are you looking at now?"

Ferris explained:

"The metal bridge that carried trains across the canal."

Suddenly, the young captain knew where the fugitives might be hiding: up on the bridge, behind the metal sides.

Calling upon some of his soldiers to join him, he began running along the towpath towards the bridge, looking for any way of scaling the steep, slippery banks leading up to where the three fugitives were hiding. It was now early evening. They hadn't stopped for a rest since their arrival. He gave the order for everyone to rest, before trying to scale the bank's slippery, steep sides. If they couldn't find a way up soon, they'd have to leave it until the next morning. It wasn't worth the risk, giving the fugitives another few hours head-start.

There was no hurry. There was nowhere they could go. And he was willing to give them a few hours more.

After checking the maps of the area, he knew for certain where the three were heading.

Over the last week, he and his men had began to respect these men, and would be sorry for the chase to end. Suddenly, they heard the rumbling of a train – as it passed over the bridge above them.

Next morning, after a night out in the open air, Turner and his men were up early, eager to be on their way. The orders from Ferris, who had chosen to go somewhere more comfortable than the hard ground for the night, had been to wait for them. By the time they arrived, and had been helped up he steep bank, the three fugitives were well away.

While Captain Turner, on the orders from Karl Ferris, had decided to rest for the night, the three fugitives after resting awhile behind the iron sides of the bridge, were travelling quickly alongside the train track, passing two small pools. On their left was a small stone bridge spanning the canal and Tom suggested that they should leave the track. but Jim, who had been leading them, thought it over and then, and looking at Len's old survey map, wanted to see if the rail track or canal would show them the way to go, or if it would take them anywhere near, the zone. They needed to know which was the quickest as their time was running out , it would not be long before they were caught. Tom soon found where on the map they were: they were still in the area known as Lapworth.

He found it difficult to find the area where they wanted to go, they had crossed so many fields and roads, he had no idea in what direction they were heading.

Tom began rummaging through his bag. Eventually he found what he had been looking for: the piece of paper that Len had drawn with the canals and places on.

"Ken and Len must have got together taking notes of the places they passed through," he said, going through Len's bag he found his little notepad and realised.

Every time they had changed direction, they had written it all in the pad, now there was a chance they could retrace their route.

But neither of them could remember what they said, what all the squiggly lines were for, nor could they make out where any of them led.

But when they compared Ken's map it all fell into place.

So while Rose rested by the side of the track, Tom studied what would be the best way to go, Jim had decided to take a little walk down the track to see what direction it took. One hundred metres along the track, it seemed to turn away from the direction in which they thought they wanted to go. They had promised if it was possible they would let those left at the zone know what they had found and what It was like.

Now he had come to a much smaller bridge which again crossed over another lane. It seemed that the whole area was criss-crossed with canals, roads and rail tracks, all crossed with little stone bridges, all hidden amongst this dense forest.

The lane below seemed to follow the direction of the canal, and looking at their rough map it seemed to take them in the direction they wanted to go, so Tom and Rose suggested that they try the lane.

Jim had wandered a little further on investigating the canal that went off in a different direction altogether, where the rail tracks crossed once again a little further along.

Tom and Rose watched as Jim walked along the track, wanting to see where the tracks would lead them.

While he carried on walking along the track, Tom and Rose stayed where they were, watching him.

Tom could not have argued, the reason why they escaped was to explore, to see what it would be like to wander around as you liked, just to be able taste their freedom for a little while longer.

He had only walked one hundred metres when they heard in the distance a rumbling sound, coming along the track from behind them. It seemed to be getting nearer and nearer.

They shouted at the top of their voices to warn him.

He could not have heard them. He just carried on walking.

Tom and Rose had just stepped off the track, when the train rushed past. The noise was terrifying.

They never heard nor saw the train hit him, not until the train had passed and the noise had subsided.

Did the two dare come out from the safety of the trees to go and find Jim, hoping that he too had jumped clear in time?

Minutes later, they found him lying two or three metres away from the track by the side of a pool amongst the bulrushes, where the force of the impact had thrown him.

He wasn't dead, but by the look of the injuries he'd sustained, they knew that he didn't have long to live.

Rose cradled Jim's head in her lap. Tom couldn't stop the tears running down his cheeks.

The pain in his chest was something he'd never felt before, as if his heart had been torn out.

This man had become more than just a friend. Not like Mark and Phil, or that couple they had watched in the field a day or two back, it was something stronger.

Oh, if only he knew the word to describe the bond that had grown between them.

Rose's sobs were uncontrollable. Their friend was dying in her arms.

Tom knelt down beside them.

Neither of them thought nor cared about the consequences if those soldiers caught up with them.

Suddenly they realised he had opened his eyes,

watching them. He smiled clutching both Rose's and Tom's hands, telling them: "No regrets."

Closing his eyes he had taken his last breath.

They moved the body out from the bulrushes so that it would easily be spotted before Tom and Rose moved off swiftly down the lane. Tom now wanted to put as much distance between them and those soldiers chasing after them.

The death of Jim had taken its toll on them both.

Rose began to fall behind; Tom knew that they wouldn't be able to continue for much longer. He waited until she was by his side and suggested that they stopped for a rest, and finish off the remaining food.

By the time they had finished the last of the food, it was dark.

If they decided to keep on the move now they could easily get lost. And as there was not a sound coming from those in pursuit, they decided to stay there for the rest of the night, and make an early morning start. It would be Tom's tenth day out here roaming around the countryside, maybe it would be his last. He hadn't told Jim or Rose that he to had been feeling sick a couple of times like Ken and Len.

By mid-morning the next day Turner and his men had been searching the towpaths on both sides of the canal for a way up the steep sides of the banks leading to the bridge. It had taken another fifteen minutes before they found the way up, the steps on the opposite side of the canal had been well hidden. Only Captain Turner and Ferris went ahead with a couple of soldiers scrambling up the steep slope towards the bridge. They had heard the train rush past the evening before and quite expected to find at least a couple of corpses when they reached the top, but to their surprise there was none. It was only when they had walked along a little did any signs become apparent that something tragic had happened here, and when one of his men began to jest and make fun of the sight that now greeted them, Captain Turner lost his temper and threatened to have the man court- martialled. Neither was Ferris too happy as they had both grown to respect all of the escapees.

"At least one of them must have been killed with the amount of blood that's around," the young captain stated.

It was when they had walked a few metres on that they found the body, but there was no sign of the other two.

Looking over the area, Turner tried to think what they would do, what were they thinking, how would they decide which path to follow? He knew their destination was to go back to where they had escaped from, but his job was to keep them moving in that direction, force them into the trap that was awaiting them.

Margaret Storrs had stayed with the others at the governor's residence, where accommodation had been set aside for them. Back at the Work Zone the trap had been set, so all they had to do was to sit and wait for the last two to show. She felt quite pleased with herself, she had heard that another body had been found dead.

It would soon be over.

Maybe there could be a recommendation and a promotion at the end of the day? Caroline did not bother, she wanted to get back and do a post-mortem on the two men who had died mysteriously.

She was very concerned why they had died. There were no wounds, just those marks on their arms and bodies. There was something about them: she tried to recall where she had seen any reference to similar marks and as she pictured the marks on the man's body the hairs on the back her neck began to stand up. It concerned her and she began to wonder if there was any connection between how they had died, and the family. Or was it a pure coincidence?

The more she thought about it, the more concerned she became.

The young police inspector turned to Yvonne, and asked:

"Do you or John have any idea why those men would want to return to the place they'd just escaped from?"

She continued: "They must know that we'll be waiting for them."

Yvonne took her time in answering. Eventually she said: "They knew full well what was intended.

"They only wanted to get back there before they were killed. I'm not quite sure why. It could be that they're going back to try and get in touch with those still remaining in the building. But that's just a thought."

"Does Margaret Storrs realise that you think this is possible?" the inspector asked.

The concerned look on her face told Yvonne she

wasn't quite sure what would happen to those still living in the zone, and all the others around the country.

Yvonne felt uneasy as the young inspector stood watching her; the look of puzzlement written on her face and in her body language as if she was thinking of a way to ask a difficult question.

"Did you recognise that old couple's handyman?" asked the inspector, awaiting for Yvonne's reply; however, none was forthcoming.

The inspector continued:

"The coloured man, had you seen him before?

"Because he seemed to know you, I could tell by the way he looked at you. when Margaret and John were outside, you were in the kitchen. I'm not going to ask where he knows you from, but I can guess that he was, perhaps, one of the escaped prisoners?"

Before Yvonne could answer, and as if she had heard her name being mentioned, Margaret Storrs came up to join them with all her followers coming up behind, with Caroline a noted absentee. She had gone with the three bodies to the morgue, still unhappy at not knowing how they had died. Hopefully she would find out in the next hour or two.

As the four soldiers that had stayed with the captain moved off as fast as they could in pursuit of the two remaining fugitives, the captain had taken a gamble that they would have chosen the lane rather than the rail track because firstly it took them in the right direction, and secondly he didn't think they would fancy the track after what had happened to their friend.

How far ahead they were he had no idea, but hopefully they should have caught up with them soon if they stuck to the lane. He didn't think they would risk entering the woods even during the day.

The noises had already begun to echo around the forest and even the armed soldiers were getting edgy; Turner could see it in their body language. He began to feel the same uneasy feeling he had before as they moved along the narrow lane, it felt as if eyes were watching them, hiding amongst the trees, nobody knew what lay ahead.

Ahead by just two kilometres hidden away in the undergrowth away from the narrow lane, Tom had told Rose that he would like to be back at the outer perimeter fence by tomorrow. This would be his tenth day of freedom and hopefully the sun would be shinning. Rose could not imagine what the difference the sun would make.

He had been studying the old map and had chosen the place where he thought would be the best possible location to send the message. Joe had already written it using a notepad, putting down a series of dots and dashes and he'd shown them all how to send it.

Realising that he might not make it till the end, he wanted to get there as soon as they could.

It was then Tom realised that out of the eleven he was the only one left. He wanted to keep that promise they had made and wondered if they had given up waiting to hear, and if there had been any reprisals.

What he had missed was their comradeship and what

had happened since they had escaped, back there inside the zone.

But for now it was time to keep moving. He hated the thought of being caught now when they were so near.

Both were hungry. They had not eaten since they'd finished the last of their food that morning, and all they had managed to find was the blackberries along the hedgerow.

Tom's stomach rumbled, he hadn't felt too well since yesterday but didn't want to say anything to Rose, He knew that it wouldn't be long before he'd be caught.

His only wish was to make it back so that he could send the message, and that they would show mercy on Rose. She was an innocent victim in all this.

They had stopped to have a short rest and pick a few berries to eat, when they heard rustling in the bushes. Something was rushing towards them, and the only weapon they had to protect themselves with was the old rusty rail that he'd carried with him since killing Rose's attacker.

Now the blood had dried, but he still remembered the feeling; he didn't like it one little bit, and doubted if he could ever do it again, maybe to protect Rose. All of a sudden the bushes parted, and Tom recognised the man standing in front of them. He was one of the scavengers that had been their guide when they first entered the forest. What on earth was he doing here?

In his hands he held two parcels which he offered to Tom, yet his eyes were fixed on Rose, unsure what to say.

His eyes were full of doubt questioning who she was.

Seeing this, Tom explained who she was, and why she was there.

Accepting Tom's explanation, the stranger said that he had brought a couple of parcels in one there was some food, the other contained a vacuum flask with a hot drink.

Then he explained: "For the last day, since your friend's accident with the train, we have been watching your progress.

"You may have guessed that the main party of those pursuing you have headed back to wait for you there, but there are a few still on your tail.

"The two things in your favour are that they have no idea where around the perimeter you are heading, and to cover that area would take far more men than they have, and the second is that the group following you thought that you would be travelling along the lane."

But the young captain had soon realised that you had risked the cover of the trees after all.

Taking a look at the map the stranger, who had made no attempt to introduce himself, asked where they intended to go. Seeing that both looked at him suspiciously, he explained that he had been instructed to guide them to wherever they wanted to go.

So with that all three settled down to enjoy whatever was in those parcels before starting their way through the trees led by their new guide.

The morning was clear, there wasn't a cloud in the

sky. There was a warmth in the air. It even made Tom feel better.

They had packed what food they had left for later, together with all their odds and ends.

There was quite a distance to go, so with the stranger leading the way and Rose following behind, they were going at a far greater pace than they would otherwise have wanted. But he seemed to know where they were, and in what direction they should be going, so without a word they followed (they had no choice).

At first Tom thought that he recognised some of the paths they were using, but amongst the trees and shrubs they passed the occasional ruin and he had no idea where they were. He wasn't worried.

All of a sudden they reached a narrow stream, at which point their guide took a swing to the left. This time they were going with the flow of water. Now it did feel familiar he felt that he knew this stream, every pebble that he stepped on. Trying to keep up the pace sometimes was difficult because of the slippery surface of pebbles on the stream's bed.

Occasionally one of them would slip and after following the stream's path for an hour, by the time they stepped out of the water onto dry land the two of them were soaked and were grateful for a rest.

Their sure footed guide just smiled.

Tom told Rose that he recognised the stream as the one that had guided had taken them before, and getting wet before. They both laughed at that. All morning they had been on the move and there were places where they broke out from the cover of the trees into open pastures, where In the warmth of sun the stranger allowed them to take a short rest.

By mid-afternoon the clouds had begun to gather and the journey was beginning to take its toll on Tom. Earlier on he had started coughing and now it was getting so bad Rose had spotted specks of blood mixed in the mucous. Rose kept pleading with the guide to let Tom rest, but the stranger kept them moving saying: "I want to get to your destination by early evening so I can return to my camp before it's too dark."

Adding: "I'm sorry but if I'm found out here there would be some very awkward questions to be answered. If they ever thought we had helped you, they would take it out on all of us in the camp. Nobody would say a word in our defence because they would say we had helped the escaped convicts."

They understood now why he was so worried, and in so much of a hurry to get back to the camp so, after a few minutes rest, they were back on their feet, setting off through the trees and bushes sometimes following the paths sometimes not. The pace was relentless.

Not one more word of complaint passed their lips.

Suddenly Tom realised that they had been walking up a slight incline. The going was becoming harder and harder. Somehow he knew they weren't very far away from their destination.

All they had to do now was to find the best place to send the message. Now darkness was creeping in quickly, it was a race against time because tomorrow may be too late. They probably knew the two of them were there. Plus Tom could feel himself getting weaker with every step he took. Suddenly there it was, the gap in the trees up ahead. Not too far to go he thought, remembering looking through their little home-made telescope. This was the place, "Thank god" he muttered to himself, clutching the little red book, which was still in his pocket.

Turning to their guide, Tom told him that it was time for him to be on his way before it was too late. After Tom had thanked him for his trouble and wished all those in his group all the best for their future, their new friend wished them all the best then turned, and headed back into the trees the way they had come. Waving goodbye, Tom and Rose looked on, sorry to see him go.

They knew that if he left it too late, then even he could easily become lost, or run into one of the soldiers. With so many soldiers around, the chances of being caught, as the night grew darker, became greater.

When their friend had disappeared into the trees the two of them began to look for the spot that Tom had found on the map. He had remembered the first day he had first spoken to his friends, when he looked through that telescope at those flashes of light between the gap created by the fallen trees.

Slowly making their way along the perimeter fence clearing away a path with their bare hands, they soon came across the fallen trees. But now it was late, there was no sun to send a message, there was nothing they could do but to settle down for the night.

Opening the vacuum flask of warm liquid, it's warmth would help to keep the evening cold out.

After eating the last of the food, Tom pointed the silhouette of the building that had been his home for twenty six years, they could make the lights through the windows, he could imagine his friends working or just laying about. As the night went on and the evening mist came down, they lay down on the ground, wrapping blankets tightly around themselves. Now in the darkness, without the sun's warmth, they were feeling the chill of the night. Tom just lay there thinking over the last few days, if it had all been worth the lives of all his friends. Through the gap in the trees he could just make out the lights of the two top floors of his building. He could imagine all those inside going about their chores.

He thought about Jacob, had he been able to fool his pursuers? He hoped he had so then at least one of them may be able to tell people about those still locked up, so it would be worth it.

He had just closed his eyes when he felt Rose slip under the blanket, before could say a word she pressed a finger to his lips. She pressed her body close to him and he realised that she was completely naked.

He had never before experienced the softness and the warmth of another body so close, then he remembered the time when she had run to him, flinging her arms around him. At first the feeling was of confusion, remembering the disappointment when she had pulled away.

Then their lips met and the overwhelming feeling of excitement slowly and softly overtook both bodies.

Waking up the next morning, Tom had never been so happy. The sun was shining over the same buildings that only a few days ago they had been so eager to escape from. He never wanted to go back there and he knew that he never would. And he now knew for certain that they were more than just talking machines: they were good men.

No matter what happened now, he knew that this would be his last day. He felt the illness eating away inside. There were no regrets though.

Leaving Rose to sleep, he slipped out from under the blanket. With the piece of broken mirror and the notepad recovered from his little bag, he began to send the message Joe had written: it was just a few words to tell them of their experiences, that he was the only one left and soon he too would be dead. But it was a beautiful land and that freedom is always worth fighting for, no matter what the cost.

It seemed like an eternity and he was just about to give up, thinking that something had happened or they too had given up waiting, when a series of flashes came to acknowledge and to thank him.

Happy that the promise had been kept, he felt pleased with himself. Suddenly he heard Rose steer behind him, taking a quick look and to his horror, he shouted a warning, but it was too late.

Standing as naked as the day she was born, stretching her arms above her head as if she was trying to catch the morning sun.

Tom marvelled at the beautiful sight standing there, he had never seen anything so beautiful, only for a second was he allowed the pleasure. A moment later where her left breast had been, a large dark hole appeared and a dark red line began to run down over the slight bulge of her stomach. She stood there for a second with eyes and mouth wide open yet no sound came from her mouth, and a look of fear and terror in her eyes.

Tom moved to catch her and stop her toppling over onto her face. Cradling Rose's body in his arms, he was unable hold back the tears that were running down his cheeks and the sound that came from his mouth was that of a wild animal. He had never thought he would ever feel such pain again since Jim's death, it was as if someone had ripped out his heart.

"Why?" he muttered under his breath. She'd done nothing wrong and was no threat to them. Yet they had killed her in cold blood. Why?

He could feel the anger building up inside. If only he could do something to avenge her. But there was nothing he could do.

In a fit of rage, he vented his frustration. With clenched fist, he flung his arms in the air, swearing revenge, not even hearing the cracks of the rifles as four or five bullets found their mark, throwing him to the ground. Blood flowing from his wounds he crawled over to where Rose's body lay, then reaching into his trousers to retrieve the little red book its pages were brown with age, the gold title pressed into the red leather. Slowly he read the title, HOLY BIBLE. He had found it all those years ago when he was just a boy, he had taken it with him when they had escaped, he had not read it for days, now holding it tightly in his hands he read a line. Pressing her body close to his, tears running down his face, the pain of the bullets were nothing compared to that of losing Rose. In their short time together, they had become soulmates, whispering into her ear a few words he read.

*Wheresoever you shall go, I shall go. Wheresoever you shall dwell, I shall dwell. Your people shall be my people. Your god shall be my god.* Wrapping her naked body in the blankets, he waited for them to come. He knew they would not be long but he had one more thing to do before he died so he waited.

Down in the valley outside the gates that opened into the zone the young captain had been attracted by the flashes up on the hill, just where the trees had been blown by last winter's storms.

As he watched through binoculars Rose's silhouette could clearly been seen in the brightness of the sun.

Yvonne looked on, fascinated by the spectacle. John had been watching the soldiers, taking up different positions. He knew what was about to happen. But before Turner could shout for them not to fire he heard the shots echo over the valley. In horror Yvonne screamed as she turned to see what was happening.

When Tom stood up and his silhouette appeared, Margaret Storrs came over and it was she who had given the order for the soldiers to fire. Thirty minutes later the group arrived at what looked like a battle zone.

Both bodies lay side by side, Tom still held Rose tightly as the group moved around the two bodies.

Margaret Storrs first checking Rose then Tom for any signs of life, as she went to feel for his pulse she saw the little red book, that he held in his hand. Taking it from the dying man she gave it a quick look through then cast it aside, leaving it there to rot amongst the leaves.

Only then she realised that he was still alive, he had opened his eyes looking, surveying all those around him, clasping the dead girl's hand in his. The look of hate in those eyes was obvious.

Taking out the box carrying the syringe Caroline had given her, Margaret wanted to finish the job that she had been sent to do.

So filled with confidence that she would be well rewarded on her return to the capital, she had not realised that though he was dying he had lifted himself onto his elbow, till his face was so close to hers their noses were nearly touching.

What was going to happen next, she was horrified not knowing what his intentions were, she called out for the soldiers.

He only spoke to say three words, but those words were spat out with such venom her face was sprayed with blood and spittle. The words were telling them all to "Go to hell."

As the liquid from the syringe began to take effect. Tom lay back, his arms holding the only one he had loved, even though he could not explain it.

In his dying seconds he thought of something else

he had read, a few lines of a poem by someone named Shelley.

*If the mountains kiss high heaven, and the waves they clasp one another, no flower would be forgiven, if it should disdain it's brother. And if the sun should clasp the earth, and the moonbeams kiss the sea, what are all these kisses worth, if thou kiss not me.*

If this was the price he had to pay for these past ten days, and after last night he knew what they all had been missing locked away all those years in those buildings, he had no regrets.

With one last effort he kissed his one love on her lips, his last breath. Standing by watching the spectacle, the little group could not help but feel touched for they realised that they were the ones missing the one thing that separated them from animals – compassion.

Yvonne felt tears running down her cheeks as she stood by and watched the two bodies entwined together. Yet these were not tears of sadness, they were of joy, because she realised that this pair had found in the short time they were together the one thing that most of the people here would never find, and that was real love.

There was something in the girl's arms clutched tightly to her damaged breast. Yvonne bent down to have a closer look and realised it was an old battered teddy bear. Where on earth would the girl have got that? Wandering around, John came across Tom's bag and soon found the book that Tom had found at the little smallholding where the family had died. It was the man's diary telling the sequence of events leading to their deaths. Margaret Storrs saw him and asked what it was that he had found but before he could reply, she snatched it from his grasp, quickly putting it away In a shoulder bag.

She was hoping that no-one else had noticed but she was too slow, Jillian Dove and Karl Ferris had seen John pick the book up. The inspector demanded to know what it was, and if it could be evidence if there was a inquest into the matter.

"I'm not quite sure what it is, but until I've had Dr Caroline have a look first – we cannot be too careful can we? Then it will be those down in the capital to decide, is that not right Karl?" said Margaret, still confident that she would be rewarded.

The young inspector knew she was beaten, for now anyway.

While the others were busy, John had been thinking over those flashes of light that he had noticed between the trees. Was it just a coincidence they looked to be in a uniform sequence, and coming from the direction of the buildings too?

Eleven men and a young girl had died. Why and what had they done to be hunted and killed?

Were they killed to hide the truth? But as an old prime minister, Winston Churchill, had once said: "The truth sometimes must be protected by a bodyguard of lies."

But all that is legal is not just. And all that just is not legal. If they thought for one minute that this was the end, how wrong could they be? It was only the beginning to the end.

# 17

Two weeks later John was sitting in the garden taking things easy, watching Yvonne pottering around the garden, pruning some of the roses. Even in those old trousers of his she used around the house, that were just a little too big, she would keep them up by tying an old tie of his around her waist. It worked to a point but every so often they would begin to slip over her hips, then John could glimpse the top of her pants, or even the cheeks of her bottom. It was these times he that he enjoyed most. It was the beginning of autumn but the sun was still quite warm. it had been two lovely weeks and both of them were quite tanned.

Since their experiences over the last few weeks, they were just getting over being witnesses to the killings of the fugitives. John was playing with the idea of going to give Yvonne a hand at watering a few plants, or collecting the last of the plums off the small tree they had planted when they had first moved in six years ago.

Tonight it was his turn to start the dinner, he had just stood up trying to make his mind up when he heard the buzzing of the communication system. After ignoring it for a few minutes he realised they were not going to give up, whoever it was sounded impatient to get in touch. He remembered the last time, and a cold shiver went down his back.

Entering the cool shade of their cottage with its low ceilings and the oak beams, it was said that the cottage was six centuries old, well before all literature had been abolished or hidden away.

As he entered through the modern glass patio doors (they were the only things that Yvonne would allow to be changed so as she would have the full view of the garden) the whole system came to life.

John immediately recognised the man facing him on the screen as Mark Sykes: the Director of Production. They had met several times over the last month or two, he was the one that had explained the significance of all the different coloured flags stuck on the map when he and Yvonne had been called to the city the second time.

He still looked as if he was going for an audition for a modelling job: the suit he was wearing looked as Immaculate as the first time they had met, his chin stay beard looked as if it had been recently trimmed.

Yet the look in his eyes, and when he spoke John knew something was seriously wrong.

After the formalities had been done and Sykes had asked how both Yvonne's and himself had been, he told John that he wanted them to be on the first train in the morning without fail to the city centre. Someone will be there to pick them up.

Not waiting for any objections the screen went blank. Wondering what he was going to say to Yvonne, he turned to find that she was already standing in the doorway, and had heard the conversation.

So again having to rise early and make their way to the station, and again not knowing what it was they had done, or what they were supposed to do. On arriving at the city's main station waiting for them was the same buggy as when they had first arrived. Travelling from the station only took a few minutes. Everywhere they looked, people were out going to and from, walking to work, shopping, or just enjoying a coffee at outside tables. No-one took the slightest interest at the buggy or its passengers.

As the buggy pulled up outside the main doors they were met by a soldier so heavily armed and protected that anyone would think the place was on the verge of being invaded, nor could they tell if he was smiling to greet them or scolding behind the thick visor.

John wondered if he was one of the soldiers that had been on the chase after the fugitives, just a couple of weeks before.

Without a word he beckoned for them to follow along the corridors until arriving at the same two huge doors as before. They seemed to open automatically as they approached and entering the same large room they had just a few weeks ago, John wondered if the map would still be hanging behind the doors.

At first they were left standing there, they thought the room was empty until John turned and saw him standing studying the map, surely he had heard them arrive.

When he did eventually turn, he walked over to the large table that seemed to dominated the centre of the room, without even acknowledging them. Then and only when he had sat down did he speak.

"Sit yourselves down. I think we know each other by now? Would you like some refreshments?" He talked as if they were about to discuss a business deal, not even bothering to enquire about their journey, but his body language told them to wait and see what this was all about.

Declining his offer, the two of them made their way over to the table and John noticed the dirty little diary, the one he had he had found on one of the fugitives of had been carrying – it was lying on the table in front of him.

Sykes asked John: "Is it the one you found in the prisoner's bag?"

John wondered if it had anything to do with them being called here and was in two minds whether to ask – what a coincidence if it had not, and it had been just left there lying on the table.

Sykes saw his interest in the diary, and when he spoke his whole body seemed to slump into the chair, his face had now lost the look of confidence it had when they had first met.

Now he had the look of a man too frightened to ask a question, because he didn't want to know the answer.

"Do you remember Margaret Storrs and Dr

Caroline?" His eyes went from one to the other as if searching for a different answer to a different question.

"Of cause you must do."

Yvonne could see the man certainly had something on his mind.

"And you also must have noticed their absence?" He quickly added Was this a trick question. He knew damn well they would, who would forget those two?

When they said they remembered both he seemed to pull himself together, then told them that both had been taken to a private hospital over a week ago, and were pronounced dead two days later. Also that three of the guards that were on that expedition had also died.

"Have you any idea what they died of?" asked Yvonne, "and what about Inspector Dove and Karl Ferris? Are they also dead?"

"No, they're both fine, but still in quarantine with our young captain and all his men. We are not quite sure yet what we are dealing with, so they will remain there until we know.

"We are doing some tests but that's why you are here. We wanted to see if you are both feeling well, no ill effects?

"What about that old couple and their handy man, are they alright?" Yvonne asked.

"Because now the thinking is that all of you may have come into contact with some kind of plague, or a tropical disease, and it looks like the old couple are not effected.

"What kind we have no idea yet."

Reaching across the table for the book, he asked them: "Have you any idea what the man meant when he wrote 'It's back, god help us'?" flipping the pages over until he came to the one he was referring to, and pointing to the phrase in question.

By their looks Mark Sykes could tell that they didn't. John confirmed it when he said that Yvonne had not seen the book and he had not seen what had been written inside. And that he had only just picked it up when Margaret had taken the book from him, before he had time to open it.

"So may we have a look and see what the man could have meant?"

Leaning across the table, Sykes pushed the diary towards John as if it were a bomb.

John positioned the little book between himself and Yvonne, so they could both read it together.

At first it was of no interest to them, only the daily running of the farm, so skipping through the pages until they came to the pages in question they began to read how the two youngest children had found an old tramp lying amongst brambles. He was very ill, he waved them away, and had warned them all to stay away, but they thought him too ill to be left, so the family had taken him home and looked after him.

But even with all their care the poor man died on the third day. The man had taken the body well away from the farm, and buried him in the woods where they hoped no-one would disturb the grave, so at least now he could rest in peace.

After four days the first of the children went down with it, then the second by the end of the week all the children were sick, and they had just buried the first of the children.

The dates in the book were one week before the bodies were discovered by the fugitives. It described how they had all died, but not what it was that killed them.

Putting the book down on the table, John had noticed some marks on the pages concerned. He asked Sykes about them, the reply worried him.

"We are doing some tests, we believe that the man was already ill and may have been coughing while writing the entries."

"Do you mean that's his mucus? If it is, then why has no-one ordered the book to be tested or locked away safe until we know?" The three moved slowly pushing their chairs away from the table, as if the book was going to blow up in front of them.

The stark reality and significance at what could be lying in front of them terrified all three, and they could not understand why no-one had realised the danger before.

"By the way, there's something else, before I forget," Sykes went on.

"Eleven men escaped, yet only ten have been accounted for. Six were killed and one was killed by the train. We don't know what the other three died of.

"So the question is: where's the eleventh? And was he with them when they found the family?

"If he was, has he been infected? Worst of all is he

wandering around the countryside spreading whatever it is, or could he be lying dead somewhere?"

"In that book it says something about the old man, who the family had found that died, and that he had found a yellow bag containing some swabs and needles. The question is: has his grave been found and what about the bag?" Yvonne asked, worried that something very important had been missed. Yvonne's voice was full of anger with the thought of so many people's lives having been put in danger over a few men being chased over the countryside.

"Wherever he is, we've got to find him soon," Sykes added, still referring to the escaped fugitive. "But all that can wait. There are more important things at moment to be sorted, because if this is the some kind of plague that caused the deaths of so many all those years ago, and has been lying around dormant for the past two centuries.

"Another question, if this was the cause for the disappearance of so many people then how is it that we've gone so long without us knowing anything about it and why, or how, have so many of us survived?" said John.

There was a few minutes silence, while the significance of what had just been said struck home.

It was Yvonne who broke the silence.

"I think I know what the man meant by god help us," she said, and they all nodded in agreement.

Yvonne remembered the old couple living in the lock keeper's house, and their helper. She was sure she had seen him before, when they had visited the buildings the first time, or had he just looked like him because of his colour? She felt that the couple were quite happy having him there to help. The more she thought about it the more it worried her. She hadn't said anything back then. Had she been wrong, should she say something now? She decided that when they get out of here, she would cycle along the towpaths towards Lapworth and check on the old couple and see if they were alright, and still happy about the situation.

They could tell there was something else on this man's mind. It was the way he kept shuffling through his papers.

It wasn't until he'd put them all away, did he start to explain that it had been decided that it would be necessary to send someone into the archives to see if there was anything there – to give an idea what they were up against.

And how or if were they able to cure it.

"It as been decided that, as both of you are Psychoanalyst and with a little bit of luck you may be able to siphon out something that will help us, from amongst all these papers. Both of you will be allowed or, should I say, be taken blindfolded to one of the major archives where all the records are kept. You won't be allowed to take anything in, and you won't be able to take notes, nor bring anything out. Understood?"

"When will we be expected to go?" asked John.

Now they knew why they had been summoned.

"In the morning, transport will pick you up at 08:00. You have three to four days to find anything of interest.

There'll be everything that you need down there. So, just bring your personal things, such as toiletries Is that clear?

"It's important you understand… that I can't be held responsible for the consequences of you not following these instructions."

He turned and started to walk towards a door at the far end of the room, without another word.

"By the way what will happen to that missing man when you find him, because now that you have brought it to the attention of the media and the police, surely there are going to be questions asked?" If Yvonne thought that by bringing the matter up it would have a reaction, she would have been disappointed.

Sykes with his hand still holding the handle of the door, just turned a little to look directly at Yvonne, and in his calm and quiet voice said:

"Maybe that would be for the best. By the way there is something else I would like to explain to you both, but it will have to wait for another day." Without another word he opened the door and was gone.

Yvonne couldn't help but respect the man.

As they walked out of the building into the sunlight, John turned to Yvonne and said:

"I think Mark Sykes may have slipped up when he had said 'down there'. If he was right It could mean that we may be heading underground but where, that is the question?"

If that was the case Yvonne could hardly hold back the excitement at the thought of being able spend time amongst the archives. Even though nothing may be brought out, the thought that they will have a chance to go through papers and books that have been hidden away for decades.

"Even if we cannot discover what had happened or why it didn't wipe out civilisation completely, it would be worth knowing and we may find out the truth at what really did happened." Yvonne couldn't help herself.

As John looked away in his thoughts she asked: "What are you thinking?"

"Oh, I just keep thinking about some flashes of light that I glimpsed, while everybody was too busy looking for that poor couple. They seemed to pass from where the man and girl were camping towards the building, and I'm sure I saw flashes coming from the building.

"I don't know why or what they were, but I cannot stop thinking that they were more than the sun's reflection shining on just pieces of glass or bright metal, nor were they some figment of my imagination. Were they messages of communication being sent between them, if so what were they saying to each other?"

Then they both knew the answer to why the fugitives had bothered to return to the place they had escaped from.

The next morning, Yvonne and John returned to the office.

Mark Sykes was at the main door, waiting for them.

They had been booked into a local hotel to save time.

"When are we leaving?" asked John.

Sykes glanced at his watch.

"Right now," came the sharp reply. "Transport's on its way.

"Everything you need for the three days will be there for you: food, drinks and even a change of clothes."

True to his word the transport arrived a minute later – an electric people carrier with the windows blacked out so they would not be able to see where they heading.

As they headed out of town there was an occasional hum of the traffic outside but it didn't take long before they were out, deep into the Warwickshire countryside, where they stopped for a toilet break.

Looking around John wondered if he could get some idea as to where they were, and as they walked over towards the restaurant toilets, he looked out over across the open fields.

Everything seemed more organised in the surrounding fields, with their well-trimmed hedgerows still holding on to a few blackberries, and wide open spaces rather than the dense forests of the north.

In the distance John could see the corrugated iron sheds of pig farms.

It was not the hedgerow or the sun that John was interested in, but the shadows.

He checked the direction of the shadows, and their length. Now he had some idea in which direction they were going, but where on earth could hold all the archives underground for so long without being discovered?

It could be anywhere on the south coast. It was no good, it could be anywhere.

Back in the vehicle and on the move, John explained

to Yvonne that he believed they were heading south. He didn't think that it would be too long before they would reach their destination.

"Where do you think we're being taken?" she asked.

"Well I believe we are heading south on the old A34 because I noticed an old sign by the side of the road when we stopped. I think we are somewhere near Newbary, so my guess is we are heading towards Portsmouth or Southhampton."

With the windows blacked out, they settled down to rest for the remainder of the journey, not able to see any of the places they passed through.

Sometimes they would be forced to stop, it was then they were able to hear the chatter of the people outside.

For the next hour they travelled south. Neither of them said a word, sometimes looking at each other, going over in their minds all that had happened over the past few weeks.

It was then that John suddenly realised that the vehicle had begun to rise slowly, they were going up a very steep slope.

When the car did eventually come to rest, for awhile they sat there before disembarking. They found themselves outside a huge pair of gates between two pillars of stone and a tall hedge that went off as far as they could see. Was this just another prison?

The view around them from the other side of the muddy path was also blocked by high hedges, but the smell of the sea was obvious. So John was right, but where on top of a hill could you hide the archives?

Fifteen minutes went by. They waited and still no-one came. Only when John went over to a small concealed door set into the main gates and rang the bell, did they get any reaction.

The small door swung open and a smartly dressed armed soldier stepped out through the door into the open space. The red cap that he wore made him look efficient and his automatic rifle was pointed directly at John's chest, It was only when their driver got out of the vehicle, and thrust a sealed envelope into the soldier's free hand, and he read the instructions, did he allow the gun to lower, using it to indicate that he wished for them to follow him.

Their driver stayed where he was saying that he or someone would return whenever they were told, and that could be anytime." Jumping back into the people carrier he was off, leaving them standing there dazed.

Once through the gates, they were closed behind immediately. There in front of them was nothing but an open field; to their left there were some signs that once upon a time a house stood and they could smell freshly-cut grass, but they began to wonder why on earth had they been sent here? There was nothing here.

# 18

The sentry knew different, leading them towards the ruins, and down half a dozen steps. They soon realised that the ruins were on a much lower level than the entrance and John recognised they were the foundations of a very large house, and that it must be of some significance.

They still had no idea why they had been brought here. Positioning himself behind them, the sentry had uncovered a steel door that until now had been well hidden from their view, ordering them to stand back as they watched him undo all the locks and bolts. They stood there looking around at nothing but an open space and a little guardhouse by the gate, but in their minds they were wondering where were they being taken.

When finally the door swung open, John and Yvonne felt the hairs on the back of their necks stand on end, not knowing where they were being sent.

In front of them all they could see was a space – two metres square – only illuminated by the sunlight.

Another door to their left could just be made out in the shadows.

The sentry explained that they must enter, while he stayed outside:

"The light only comes on when the door's locked", he said. "Only then can you open the door to your left."

By way of an explanation, he added:

"This is an air-lock. It keeps the temperature and humidity inside constant." John and Yvonne entered the small space.

"Everything you need is down there."

He paused, choosing his next words carefully.

"However, if you require anything, just call. There's a phone you can use."

His tone of voice grew darker.

"But, I must remind you, that everything… and I mean EVERYTHING… must be put back."

He pointed inside the room, beckoning the two to enter.

They did so, nervously – whereupon, the door slammed shut.

The space was enveloped with bright light. They could hear the bolts on the outside being slid into place.

They inspected the steel door in front of them. It measured around 2000mm x 500mm and had a small wheel, about 200mm in diameter, in the centre.

After turning the wheel anti-clockwise a few notches, a hissing sound could be heard – as the air in both spaces mixed. The temperature was changing.

Opening the door, they understood where they were going.

In front of them, they saw the passageway, dug out of rock and burrowing deep into the depths of the hill.

After what seemed an eternity, the passage lit up by the lights fitted to the top of the tunnel every few metres going down as far as they could see, with one single handrail on each side giving them something to hold on to because the steps were also cut out of the bare rock.

After getting accustomed to the dim lights of the tunnel, they realised that the space wasn't quite big enough for the two of them so John stepped on down on to the first step, giving Yvonne room enough turn and close the door behind them without going head over heels down the steps.

"I wonder," Yvonne remarked, "who and when these tunnels were dug out and how deep they go? They seem to go on for ever."

John took his first step into the unknown and began the decent down, with Yvonne just two steps behind. The steps were well worn and quiet slippery making their progress to the bottom slow.

John nearly lost his footing several times and they were relieved after several minutes to have reached the bottom.

They were both amazed at the size of the area in front of them. It was a huge cave packed full of row after row of shelves with just narrow passages between them, packed with books, folders, files and papers, and against the walls there were hundreds of paintings of all descriptions, packed away in their protective packing, protected from any damage.

The only sound in the place, was the hum of the air conditioning units. Walking around they were overwhelmed by the size of the job in front of them. They could not have ever imagined that it would be like this, not in a million years, where on earth should they start.

To begin with they must find where they were supposed to stay. After wandering around for a while, they soon came across an area that had been set aside for them, in a small corner right at the back of one of the passages. As promised, everything they would need was there.

Even a huge map of the whole area telling them where everything had been stored and indexed in reference of date and of importance, it also showed the bathrooms and toilets.

Once they had acclimatised themselves with their quarters, both agreed that it was time to start going through the shelves. The sooner they started, the sooner they could be out of here.

Even with air conditioning it was claustrophobic.

The very thought of so many tonnes of earth above them had already started to play on their nerves.

Walking through the long passages, where would they start? There were books and papers dating back many centuries, and to go through all these would take months, let alone three days. So it was decided that the best place to start they thought, would be to go back two or three hundred years and see what the population was then and come forwards. Going along the rows of shelves reaching right up to the ceiling looking for the year 1900.

After clearing a pile of old books and papers off a nearby table, Yvonne sorted out some writing materials, while John brought some of the books, papers and files he could find, dating from 1900--1999. But after several hours with their heads stuck in book after book, even though they learned about the people who had lived and worked and about the two world war's the lose of all those young men and women, the slaughter of the men women and children when one race chose to ethically--cleans another there was nothing to tell them what had happened, or when they could not be sure if it happened around that date or years after. Also there were those natural disaster that would kill millions but still they found no answers.

After nine hours their eyes ached and their heads hurt. It was time to call it a day yet they were no nearer to finding out what they wanted.

In a corner a large refrigerator stood with all the food that they would want, even a little microwave to heat their food. When they had washed and eaten and felt a little refreshed, they went to find where they were to sleep. When they saw where they were going to sleep they laughed, because neither had slept in bunk beds since they were children.

Strangely enough it was well after 09:00 the next

morning when they woke, only because someone was banging on the door some 300 steps above. They just looked at one another, neither volunteered to go and see what all the fuss was about.

Both gave a sigh of relief when the banging stopped thinking that the culprit had left, but no sooner had they settled down for breakfast, after a quick shower, when the phone on the wall began to ring furiously. Positioned at the far end of one of the passages, Yvonne asked John to go and see what they wanted, surely they don't expect us to have any answers just yet.

Answering the call John found that the place was directly connected to the capital, and whoever it was, they were impatient and wanting to know if there was any progress made on finding out to what had happened. They weren't too happy when he told them that they were no further forward.

So after breakfast John got stuck into a pile of old newspapers while Yvonne carried on studying official documents, books and copies of old television programs. Then while they were discussing their findings, they realised that what was often written in the papers, old films and books did not always agree with what was written in the official documents or letters.

"By the looks of things the ordinary people in the street were misled by what they were told, don't you think?" said Yvonne. John looked over from some papers he'd been studying.

"I think I read somewhere in one of those books, someone was quoted as saying that the media could be a diabolical weapon. Using the most modern forms of communication, it could forge and corrupt men's thoughts with their lies and half-truths, because a half-truth can be the most effective lie."

As he spoke, he waved his arm in the direction of a huge pile of papers. The more they delved into it, the more despondent they were, and began to think that now we've got it right, so maybe there are a few that are locked away.

"What we've read up till now, what with the wars, terrorists, murder and the thousands that were dying though starvation, looking at some photos of little boys and girls: some dying though hunger and thirst because the water companies wanted to make more profit, some through cold. Then there were those casualties of the fighting," John said, pushing away a pile of papers that he had been going through. John lent back on his chair, tears running down his cheek and said: "I've had enough, I want to be out of here."

Yvonne looked over, a look of horror on her face.

"John," she said, "don't you realise that what's happening today might be the very things that happened then, but if we cannot find the answers it could be the end of humanity as we know it. We've also got to find out how some managed to survive and to overt many more innocent people dying."

For the next two days, going through book after book, paper after paper, and still they could not find the answers that they had been searching for.

It wasn't until late in the evening, just when they

were about to give up, that John found a brown folder stuck at the very back of a shelf. It was lying flat covered in a thick layer of dust, sealed with wax and the words in large red capitals: STRICTLY CONFIDENTIAL.

Where the other documents were all on view, this one was out of sight, hidden away, lying flat, covered by loads of old papers and dust.

Reaching over to retrieve it, John noticed some other official markings pressed deep into the wax. Looking more closely he could just make out the word "bigot", wondering what the word was doing on a official document. Confused, he called Yvonne over to see if she could make out its meaning.

Yvonne looked puzzled when she first saw the word, then she remembered something she had just been reading.

She turned towards one of the tables which still had quite a few papers still scattered all over the them, and after ruffling through the papers awhile pulled out one she was looking for a book. Quickly going through the pages, making sure it was what she wanted, she handed it to John, who still didn't understand what he was supposed to be reading.

She explained that it meant only those people who had undergone the most thorough of security checks were entitled to see 'bigot' documents.

Turning the pages until she came across the one she wanted, confirming what she had just said, the paper was dated 1972. It was the year when some of the secrets of the world 11 had been released.

Bigot had been stamped on documents so that viewing was restricted to only a certain few on the run up to the Normandy Landings.

"So this folder could be restricted also?" asked John.

Breaking the seal and untying the red ribbon holding it together, John was eager to see what could be so important that it should be hidden away from all eyes for so long.

With the folder lying flat on the table both of them stood looking at it, trying to build the courage to open it now that the seal had been broken. So now there was nothing to lose, they opened the folder and in front of them they reckoned there must have been around 200 to 300 pages.

They were just about to start study the pages properly, when suddenly the phone on the wall began ringing.

Fearing that their time was up, just when they thought that they had found something, they let it continue to ring for a while longer.

When Yvonne did eventually answer, it confirmed what they had feared. They were told they must leave immediately, and leave everything as it is.

They must not bring anything out with them. Transport was on its way and will be here shortly.

Looking at one another they tried to understand what on earth was happening, while Yvonne went to check everything had been left as they had found it John stayed to retie the folder and put it back and hide it under all the papers.

How long will it be before that folder will see the light of day again?

Before retying the ribbon John quickly went over the pages, one by one, remembering every single word, then once more just make sure. Then and only when he was sure that he had memorised every single piece of paper did he retie the red silk ribbon, placing it where they had found it, under all the papers, books and folders he even blew some of the dust over.

Making sure she wasn't carrying anything, not even a pencil, Yvonne made her way up the slippery steps to the top. She had left John finishing off while she started to make her way out.

Disappointed that they had not found anything, yet she couldn't stop thinking about that one folder. What was the word at the top of the first page, and what did it mean? She wished she could only remember.

As Yvonne reached the top step she could hear John just starting the slow ascension to the top. By the way he was panting coming up the steps, he could do with a little work out she thought to herself, and when he finally reached the little platform where Yvonne was waiting for him, he was completely exhausted.

"I wouldn't want to do that every day," he said as he closed the door behind him.

There was no time to rest, as soon as they were reunited, the outer door swung open.

The sentry instructed both of them that their transport had arrived and was waiting just outside the main gates to take them back.

Their instructions were to report back to the Midlands head office immediately, as something had come up. They were reminded that everything that they had found must, under no circumstances, be brought out. The sentry checked John over but refrained from checking Yvonne and chose just to give Yvonne a glance over, just to make sure that they had nothing hidden away.

He had been told that everything they had written must be destroyed also. The driver didn't hold back, no sooner were they sitting down in the people carrier than they were off at full speed; there would be no stopping this time, but the driver did lower the darkened windows enough for them to view the countryside as they sped past.

It wasn't long before they were sitting in front of the desk that they had been sitting at not so long ago.

Sykes sat opposite silently, reading through some papers, and again he never bothered to acknowledge them, or look up when they had entered the huge room.

Considering all the fuss, with all the staff rushing here, there and everywhere, they sat in silence waiting to be told what all the fuss was about. What was this new information that they had been told about?

Eventually the man put the papers away in a drawer and, after making sure that the drawer was well and truly locked, he turned his attention to them. Still he didn't speak, not at once, but when he did, he was deadly serious and the look on his face warned them both that he was.

"They think they know what the man meant when he wrote *'It's back, god help us'* and they have found a way to control it.

"Whatever it is, they are not letting on they do not want to cause any panic. What they have said though is that it is a kind of plague, the symptoms are flu-like with swollen lymph glands and often occur in the neck, armpits and groin region.

"In 30-60% of cases it is fatal.

"Any questions?"

"How is the plague spread?" John asked, trying to remember each page of the folder, then suddenly realising that he was checking under his own arms and neck.

"There are three ways the plague can be spread but the most infectious they say would be pneumonic, which is transmitted through the air between sufferers."

Sykes words came out slowly giving both professors time to digest what he had just said.

Both professors looked at each other trying to understand what the hell he was talking about.

Maybe after what had happened these past weeks, and what they had been reading the last two days, could it have been possible for anyone to have such a thing hidden away for so long?

But they thought it would be better not to say anything for now.

"So have you found out anything while you were down there?"

It was more of a statement rather than a question.

"By the way I must warn you, that you are still under oath, so you must never tell anyone about what you've seen these last few weeks, otherwise I will not be held responsible for the consequences.

"Also there is something else I have been instructed to tell you before you are allowed to leave, that we are still not convinced that it was the plague that was the cause of the deaths of half of the world's population nearly two hundred years ago. So you see, if this knowledge got out there would be a world-wide panic.

"But as you have not found anything that would prove or disprove this theory, then that will be the end of the matter."

When they arrived back home they were not quite sure what to make of the past few weeks, but it was good to be back home.

It had been two weeks since they had heard of the deaths of Margaret Storrs, Dr Caroline and the others who had been in contact with disease, yet they had not heard anymore; neither of them were too concerned because the less they knew the better.

Today was no different, John was sitting at the desk looking out towards the river. Through the rain he could see the ripples made by the raindrops; it had not stopped raining for the last two days and he could have sworn that the river had risen 50cm, and now everything was looking so miserable.

Yvonne stood not three metres away, she too had been watching the rain but her mind was elsewhere. She was thinking about other things, then turning to face

John she didn't quite know the best way to approach the subject that was bothering her.

He could see that there was something wrong.

"OK what's on your mind?" he asked. "Something is bothering you and for the last few days you've been so quiet. Are you worried about anything?"

"Well as a matter of fact I've been thinking about that folder we found. It was a pity we had to leave when we did, if only the transport had been a hour later we might have had time to see what was so important.

"And I've also been thinking about that man with the old couple, do you remember the coloured man? I think he was one of the fugitives, the one that was missing, and I've cycled along to the canal to check to see if they are OK."

"And how are they?"

John just smiled.

"Yes I remember him he looked rather familiar, why do you ask? But before you answer I must ask what would you say if tell you that I had opened the folder and, even better, read through the whole thing, and I now know what had happened all those years ago, but I cannot tell you because if they found out, our lives would not be worth living?

"That's why I've not spoken about it, we cannot undo what has happened in the past, and anyway who would believe us?"

Yvonne replied: "Maybe, but what's to stop you writing a book as a work of fiction? They won't know where you got the information, would they?"

"Maybe but I think that we had better leave it fore awhile don't you, just in case?" John asked wanting to know how Yvonne felt.

It would be another twelve months before John would begin to write.

Without saying another word, John settled himself back at his desk.

His fingers began to race over the keys as his photographic memory began to picture each page he had read and the pictures he had seen. He was now relieved to be able to tell people in his own way about those locked up, and what had really happened all those years ago.

He called the title of his new book C.A.B.A.L. As John's fingers danced across the keyboard.

Yvonne stood looking out at the garden, the smile only enforced her beauty. Her thoughts were on those poor boys that had died and the girl clutching the old and battered teddy, as she watched the leaves playing in the gentle breeze across the lawn.

She had often cycled along the towpaths but today she had been past the little cottage alongside the canal where she had seen the man working the docks alone. She had stopped just to ask how the old couple were. Only to be told that they had past away early in the year, The woman had died first a month later the old man, the doctor said he died of a broken heart. With the sleeves of his shirt rolled up and the front button's undone down to his waist the dark brown skin glistened with sweat, as he lead her through the little orchard, where the old couple had been laid to rest lying side by side, "This is where they loved the best no where else would be good enough for them." He had said with tears running down his cheeks.

When it was time for her to leave the looks that had been exchanged between them said that both of them knew the truth.

But like those ten fugitives the old couple are now free… free to wander through the winter's rain, and the summer's sun; from plant to plant, bush and tree… No sorrow, worry or pain.